Clint would have laughed at her overreaction if it hadn't depressed him. No matter how much he tried, he would never be able to get her to stop hating him.

"Nobody working for Luther will think it's us walking through the lot if we're acting like lovers," he explained to her. "Everybody knows how much you hate me."

Most of all him.

Maybe she took that as a challenge, because she suddenly slid her arm around his waist and snuggled against his side. He tensed now, but not with revulsion. He tensed because his body was reacting to the closeness of hers.

Rosie lifted her face to his and fluttered her lashes. "You're right," she said. "Everybody knows how much I hate you. They'd never believe I'd be doing this..." Then she reached out and ran her fingertips along his jaw as she leaned even closer to him.

* * *

Be sure to check out the previous books in the exciting Bachelor Bodyguards miniseries.

* * *

If you're on Twitter, tell us what you think of Harlequin Romantic Suspense! #harlequinromsuspense

Dear Reader,

I am so excited to share with you more stories about the Payne Protection Agency from my Bachelor Bodyguards series. If you haven't read any of the series yet, I'll quickly bring you up to speed.

Lawman Logan Payne left his job as a detective at the River City Police Department to start his own security business. His twin, Parker Payne, left his job as a vice cop to join Logan, and when he returned from the marines, their younger brother, Cooper, joined them. Cooper and Parker recently started their own branches of the agency. Cooper's team consists of all former marines, as well as their sister, Nikki Payne. Parker's team consists of all former vice cops, which is why Parker's stepfather—the new River City PD police chief—hired Parker's team to make sure a drug lord, Luther Mills, goes to trial. Mills has threatened everyone associated with his upcoming trial.

Parker hopes his team's first big assignment doesn't wind up being their last. Clint Quarters has the toughest bodyguard assignment: protecting the sole witness to a murder Luther personally carried out. The assignment is tough because not only is Luther determined to make sure Rosie Mendez doesn't testify against him, but also Rosie blames Clint as much as she does Luther for her brother's murder.

Hope you enjoy these new stories about the Payne Protection Agency as much as I've enjoyed writing them.

Happy reading!

Lisa Childs

GUARDING HIS WITNESS

Lisa Childs

HARLEQUIN® ROMANTIC SUSPENSE

Recycling programs
for this product may
not exist in your area.

ISBN-13: 978-1-335-66187-6

Guarding His Witness

Copyright © 2019 by Lisa Childs

This edition published by arrangement with Harlequin Books S.A.

For questions and comments about the quality of this book, please contact us at CustomerService@Harlequin.com.

® and TM are trademarks of Harlequin Enterprises Limited or its corporate affiliates. Trademarks indicated with ® are registered in the United States Patent and Trademark Office, the Canadian Intellectual Property Office and in other countries.

Printed in U.S.A.

Ever since **Lisa Childs** read her first romance novel (a Harlequin story, of course) at age eleven, all she wanted was to be a romance writer. With over forty novels published with Harlequin, Lisa is living her dream. She is an award-winning, bestselling romance author. Lisa loves to hear from readers, who can contact her on Facebook, through her website, lisachilds.com, or her snail-mail address, PO Box 139, Marne, MI 49435.

Books by Lisa Childs

Harlequin Romantic Suspense

Bachelor Bodyguards

His Christmas Assignment
Bodyguard Daddy
Bodyguard's Baby Surprise
Beauty and the Bodyguard
Nanny Bodyguard
Single Mom's Bodyguard
In the Bodyguard's Arms
Soldier Bodyguard
Guarding His Witness

The Coltons of Red Ridge

Colton's Cinderella Bride

Top Secret Deliveries

The Bounty Hunter's Baby Surprise

The Coltons of Shadow Creek

The Colton Marine

Visit the Author Profile page
at Harlequin.com for more titles.

For my parents, Jack and Mary Lou Childs, who
would have been married seventy years this month.
Although Mom has been gone a few years now,
I know their love is as strong as it ever was.
Their love story continues to inspire me.

Chapter 1

Feeling like he'd been called to the principal's office, Parker Payne settled nervously onto the chair in front of the desk of the new chief of the River City Police Department. The fact that Woodrow Lynch was also his new stepfather didn't help his anxiety.

Even though it had been some years since he'd been in school, Parker remembered all too well the feeling of being called to the principal's office. The anxiety that gathered low in his stomach, twisting it into knots.

He'd spent a lot of time in this office, too, when he'd worked for the River City PD's vice unit. But he'd quit the job a long time ago when his twin, Logan Payne, had resigned from being a detective in order to launch the Payne Protection Agency. Now Parker had his own franchise of the family business. He was a boss. But something about Woodrow Lynch and this office made him feel like the troublemaking kid he'd once been. Or at least like the rule-breaking vice cop he'd been.

"You're probably wondering why I asked you to meet me here," Woodrow began. The guy was family now, but the former FBI bureau chief was still intimidating as hell with his big build, iron-gray hair and stone face that revealed none of what he was thinking or feeling.

Parker, who was usually never without words, just nodded in response.

"It's because I want to hire you."

Parker's jaw dropped. "But I already have a job." His own damn business, actually—one that he loved and wasn't about to abandon to go back to a place with too many rules.

Woodrow's lips curved into a slight smile. "I know. That's what I meant. I want to hire your agency."

Panic struck Parker's heart. "Why? Is Mom in danger? Are you?" His mom, widowed for nearly two decades, had just found happiness again. Parker hated the thought of anyone putting her life or her newfound happiness at risk.

"No, not at all," Woodrow assured him. "She's fine. This is strictly business."

Parker narrowed his eyes and futilely tried to read his stepfather's unreadable face. "Why me?" he asked. "Why my agency?"

His brothers, Cooper and Logan, had their own agencies. And Logan's agency employed two of Woodrow's former special agents, one of whom, Gage Huxton, was now his son-in-law.

"It's business for me," Woodrow said. "It might be personal for you."

A chill chased down Parker's spine. He hated when things got personal, which happened all too often with the Payne Protection Agency. "How's that?"

"Luther Mills."

That was all Parker had to hear, and the heat of anger and frustration burned away that chill of foreboding. For years he'd tried to bring down the biggest drug dealer in River City—maybe in Michigan—but he'd never succeeded. Fortunately, some members of his team, before they'd left the River City PD to become bodyguards, had been more successful. Or so he'd thought. "What about him?"

"He's going to trial soon."

Parker nodded again. He knew the story; it was how one of his bodyguards had finally left the force to join his agency. Clint Quarters had quit the vice unit after Luther Mills personally killed Clint's informant. While Luther was responsible for many, many deaths in River City, he usually didn't do his own dirty work, but he'd wanted to send a message.

"Some of his phone calls from jail indicate that he's going to make sure that doesn't happen," the chief said.

"How?"

"He's put a plan into motion to take out everyone involved with the prosecution, from the eyewitness to the CSI tech and even the judge's daughter."

"How does he know…?"

"There's a mole somewhere," Woodrow replied with a heavy sigh. "I don't know if it's in my department or the district attorney's office. But because I can't trust anyone in the department, I need the help of you and your team."

"But that hit list could include some members of my team," Parker pointed out. Probably Clint…

But Clint wasn't the one who'd arrested Luther. A detective had had that honor.

Woodrow shrugged. "I don't know. He must have found another way to communicate. We just know that he wants the witness taken out first and then the rest of the people associated with the trial. There could be others…"

Parker had taken longer than his brothers to assemble his team. He'd known whom he wanted because he'd worked with them before—in the vice unit. But he'd had to work at convincing them to leave the River City PD. He didn't want to lose any of them. But if he took this assignment, he was very afraid that he would.

Luther Mills was the most dangerous criminal Parker had ever crossed paths with. And that was something, considering the number of criminals he'd dealt with in his lifetime.

Because of that, he knew he couldn't say no to the chief. Luther Mills could not get away with murder again. He had to be stopped.

He will not be stopped. Your life is in danger…

Rosie Mendez shivered as she read the message someone had slipped under the door of her apartment. She didn't need the warning to know she was in danger. But she appreciated that one of Javier's old friends must have risked his safety to deliver the message to her.

Maybe she wasn't the only one who missed her brother. Sometimes she felt as if she was. She felt so alone now that he was gone. Too soon at just twenty years old.

Eight years older than he was, Rosie had felt more like his mother than his sister most of their lives. But that hadn't been just because of the age difference. It had been because she'd been more of a mother than their mother had ever been capable of being—to either of them. So when Javier had died, she'd felt like she had lost a part of herself. The best part…

Tears stung her eyes, but she blinked them back. She'd already wept herself out over Javier's death. All the crying in the world wouldn't bring him back. But he deserved justice. So Luther Mills wasn't going to scare her off.

And maybe that was what the note was. Maybe it wasn't a well-meant warning at all. Maybe it was a threat intended to get her to run. Or at least to tell the prosecutor that she would not testify. But there was no chance in hell that she was going to let her brother's killer go free.

He wasn't the only one responsible for Javier's death. If only that other man could be brought to justice, too…

But *he* was even more untouchable than Luther Mills.

She glanced at the note again. She hadn't noticed it when she'd come home from work, and she would have walked right over it when she'd entered the apartment. The white slip of paper stood out against the dark hardwood floor. That was how she'd seen it when she stepped out of the kitchen. Someone must have slipped it beneath her door when she'd been getting a snack from the galley kitchen of her tiny apartment.

A breeze wafted through the open living room window. But it was eerily quiet for a night in this building. Where was the rumble of voices from the alley that window overlooked? People were usually hanging out back there. She couldn't even hear voices or movement from the other apartments, and the walls were paper thin.

Where was everyone? She walked up to the door and peered through the peephole—at an empty hallway.

Where was the young officer who'd escorted her home from her second shift at the hospital? Usually he was posted at her door until another officer took his place in the morning. Had he seen whoever had left that note and chased after him?

That left her completely unprotected. Not that one officer was much protection against the army that worked for Luther Mills. The drug lord could probably have had her taken out any time that he'd wanted.

What was he waiting for?

The trial was due to start soon. She wasn't the only witness, though. If she had been, the prosecutor wouldn't have even brought the case against Mills. Eyewitness testimony was too often discounted as unreliable.

Rosie would never forget what she'd seen, how her brother had been gunned down in cold blood right in front of her. Even as she'd screamed and dropped to her knees next to his bleeding body, she'd braced herself for the bullets she'd been certain would be fired into her body as well.

Instead of killing her, Luther had leaned close and

whispered into her ear, "You have Clint Quarters to thank for this…"

Thank him? She'd wanted to kill him—just like she'd wanted to kill Luther. Like the drug lord had said, Quarters was almost as responsible as if he'd pulled the trigger himself. He'd certainly been the one who'd put the target on Javier. Yet there were no repercussions for him.

He hadn't lost anything—while Rosie had lost everything. She had nothing else to lose now but her life.

She shivered again.

Where had that officer gone?

Had he been injured?

As a nurse, it was her duty to try to treat him if he was. The peephole offered only a limited view of the hallway, with its dirty beige walls and dim lights. Maybe the officer was lying on the worn vinyl floor, bleeding out just like Javier had. Despite her training as an ER nurse, she hadn't been able to save her brother. He had died in her arms.

She blinked against another rush of tears. The last thing Javier had done before he'd died was reach up and wipe away her tears. "Don't cry for me, Rosie," he'd told her.

But that wasn't all he'd said.

She couldn't think about the rest of it, though—not without getting furious. He'd wasted his dying breath on Clint Quarters. She hated the man for that almost as much as she hated him for causing her brother's death.

Despite her efforts, that fury rushed back, and the sheer force of it quashed her fears. She was not going to cower in her apartment while someone might be hurt and in need of her help. Her hand trembled slightly as she fumbled with the row of dead bolts on her battered door, but she managed to turn them all. Then she grasped the knob and pulled open the door.

And she gasped as she stared up into the unfairly good-looking face of the man she hated most—even more than she hated Luther Mills. Was she just imagining him there? Surely after she'd thrown him out of her brother's funeral he wouldn't have had the guts to seek her out again.

Would he?

The man certainly looked like Clint Quarters with his golden-blond hair and square jaw with stubble a few shades darker than his hair. He stared down at her with those deep green eyes of his.

And she trembled with the fury rushing through her body. That was all it was. After what he'd done to Javier, she couldn't feel anything else for him but anger and hatred. Her first instinct was to slam the door in his face, but before she could swing it shut he caught it and no matter how much she struggled, she couldn't move the door or him. Maybe he was made of granite.

She'd thought that before—that he couldn't be human. That he had no heart. No soul.

This is a bad idea. Clint had told Parker that the minute he'd given him this assignment. But yet he hadn't turned down his boss. Clint knew no one else would protect Rosie Mendez like he would. The only thing he'd been worried about was that she would refuse to let him protect her.

He hadn't been worried about himself. But maybe he should have been, since she was trying really hard to slam the door in his face.

Then she shoved at his chest, trying to push him back from her door. But he didn't budge. And it wasn't just because he had an assignment to carry out.

He'd made her brother a promise a long time ago. And if anything happened to her, he would be breaking that promise. Unfortunately, it wouldn't be the first promise he'd broken that he'd made to Javier.

"Go away!" she screamed at him, and her curly brown hair tangled around her flushed face. "Get the hell out of here!"

He shook his head. "I'm not going anywhere," he told her. "Not without you…"

"Have you lost your mind?" she asked, her brown eyes wide with shock. "I am not going anywhere with you. Ever!"

"You're going to die if you don't," he warned her.

"Are you threatening me?" She stepped out of her apartment and looked around him, calling out, "Officer! Officer!"

The hallway was empty but for him. The building felt empty—which only confirmed what Clint had heard.

"What did you do with him?" she demanded to know. "Where is he?"

"Who?" he asked.

"The police officer who brought me home from the hospital," she replied. She was wearing her scrubs still. They were a deep blue that complemented her naturally tan skin. But hell, Rosie Mendez would look beautiful in anything. She had—even in the somber black dress she'd worn for her brother's funeral.

"Where is he?" she asked again.

Clint shrugged. But he felt a niggling sensation between his shoulder blades. Had something happened to the police officer? Or had Luther Mills gotten to him, paying him off to look the other way or worse?

Parker had warned Clint and the other members of their team that they could trust no one but one another. The River City PD and the DA's office had been compromised. Because they weren't sure who the moles were, they couldn't place confidence in anyone.

That wasn't hard. Clint trusted few people. The hard part would be getting Rosie to trust him. Hell, that wouldn't just be hard; it would probably prove impossible.

But he wouldn't let that stop him from keeping his last promise to her brother. The buzz on the street and from the jail was that something was going down tonight to get rid of the witness.

Javier hadn't been Clint's only informant. But he'd been his best.

"We need to get out of here," Clint said, and he reached for her arm.

She jerked back. "Don't touch me!" she said, her voice shaky with fury or maybe fear.

He would never hurt her. At least, not physically. He couldn't help how he'd already hurt her. It was too late to change that, though.

Javier was gone.

She would *not* be next.

"Come on," he said, his patience with her wearing thin.

She had to know that she was in danger, especially since her police detail had mysteriously disappeared.

"We need to get out of here!"

The eerie silence had been broken by the sound of

footsteps—a lot of footsteps—heading up the stairwell at the end of the hall. That niggling sensation he'd had turned to a cold sweat that chilled his skin and his blood. He didn't need Parker Payne's mom's notorious sixth sense to know that something bad was about to happen.

"I'd rather die than go anywhere with you!" she told him. And just as she said the words, gunfire began to ring out in the hallway behind Clint.

He shoved her inside the apartment with such force that he knocked her to the floor. Then he dived in behind her, slamming the door shut.

No matter how the hell many dead bolts she had on it, turning them wasn't going to keep out the firepower coming after her. He turned only a couple before he dragged her up from the floor and tugged her toward the window.

And as bullets began to strike and penetrate the old wooden door, he wrapped his arms around her and hurled them both through that open window.

He knew it was their only hope of escape—if they could survive the fall…

Chapter 2

Luther Mills took the phone away from his ear and stared at it for a long moment. He couldn't have heard what he thought he had. The phone was a drop cell one of the guards had picked up for him. Everybody had a price.

Well, almost everybody.

"What the hell did you say?" he asked his caller to repeat himself.

"Clint Quarters showed up at her apartment first," the guy replied.

This was a new member of Luther's crew, someone he'd hired specifically to make sure this trial never took place. But he wasn't certain he could trust the man. But hell, Javier Mendez had proved to him that he couldn't trust anyone. And then when he'd put bullets in the kid, Luther had proved that anyone who dared to cross him would die.

Too bad Javier's stubborn sister hadn't learned that lesson yet. But she would. It would be the last thing Rosie ever learned.

"And before we could get to her," the guy continued, "they jumped out a window."

Clint Quarters.

He was one of those damn people who had no price. Like Rosie...

Maybe his guys had it wrong. Maybe she'd shoved Quarters out the window.

Did it matter? All that mattered to Luther was that she not testify against him. He didn't care why. And he certainly didn't care if Clint Quarters had died with her. Actually he would prefer that Clint died.

And not Rosie.

He'd always had a soft spot for her since they'd been kids in grade school together. Rosie had always been so sweet and serious and smart. That soft spot was why he'd waited so long to put out the hit on her. But running his business from jail was getting old. That was why he'd put the plan into motion to eliminate the eyewitness. It was past time that he get out again.

And there was no way in hell he was ever going to prison.

"What the hell is wrong with you!" Rosie shrieked at the crazy man driving erratically through the streets of River City. Of course, that erratic driving might have had something to do with the wound to his shoulder. Blood streaked down the leather sleeve of his torn jacket. She didn't know if he'd been shot or if he'd hurt it when he'd hurtled them both through her apartment window.

She couldn't stop shaking as fear and adrenaline continued to course through her. Her fingers trembled too much for her to even pull the safety belt across her lap. But she needed to—as he careened around a corner and her body slammed against the passenger's door. "Are you trying to kill us?"

She'd thought for certain that she was going to die when they'd catapulted through that window of her third-floor apartment. But there had been a dumpster beneath it, and somehow Clint had turned so that she fell on top of him. He was the one who'd hit whatever had been in the dumpster. She suspected he'd also hit the edge of the rusted metal bin.

"I'm trying to make sure you don't get killed," he told her through gritted teeth.

Was he gritting his teeth because he was in pain?

She should have been happy that he was, after all the pain he'd put her through. But instead she felt concern. Maybe that was just because she'd been a nurse for so long. She couldn't not react to someone who was hurt, no matter who that person was.

She glanced behind them. "Nobody's following us." She couldn't imagine how they could with the way he was driving. "Pull over."

"I am not letting you out of this vehicle," he told her—again through gritted teeth.

"What?" She didn't want out. She didn't even know where the hell they were. But his telling her that she couldn't…

Suddenly made her want out very badly.

"Are you kidnapping me?" she asked as even more adrenaline rushed through her.

"I'm protecting you," he said.

She shook her head. "You're not a policeman anymore."

He'd quit—right after Javier's murder. The detective who'd arrested Luther Mills had told her. She'd been surprised that Clint hadn't wanted Luther's arrest for himself since he'd sacrificed her brother to get it. But then she'd refused to give her eyewitness account to him. She'd refused to talk to him at all until he'd had the gall to show up at the funeral. Then she'd said plenty.

"No, I'm not a cop anymore," Clint admitted. "I'm a bodyguard."

"Well, I sure as hell didn't hire you to protect me," she said. Even if she could have afforded private security, she would not have paid for his services.

"The police chief hired the agency I work for now," he replied. "The Payne Protection Agency."

"The police chief?" she asked skeptically. He had a whole police force at his disposal. Why would he hire a private security company?

Clint shrugged and a grimace contorted his handsome face. He was definitely hurt. "Luther has information he shouldn't. He's gotten to people in the police department and the DA's office," he said.

Panic had her gasping. "The police officer who was protecting me?" What the hell was his name? Officer Maynard. She remembered now, because she'd thought Javier would have teased him about his name. And he couldn't be much older than her brother.

"Maybe," he said. "I didn't see who was shooting at us. But even if it was him, he wasn't the only one shooting. You can't trust anyone."

No. She couldn't. But she couldn't wrap her mind around that young officer trying to kill her.

"But he could have taken me out any time." A chill chased down her spine, making her tremble even more than she had been. "Why…"

"Luther gave the order that it was to happen tonight," he said.

That was why Clint had shown up at her door when he had. She shook her head. "I don't understand."

"What's not to understand?" he asked. "He doesn't want you to testify."

"But if he has me killed, he'll do time for my murder," she pointed out. "Either way, he winds up in prison."

Clint shook his head now. "He's smarter than that. He's been careful with what he's said. Nothing would be admissible in court."

"Then how can you be sure?" she asked.

He took his gaze from the street to stare at her for a moment. "After the shooting, how can you ask that?"

"Maybe they were shooting at you," she suggested. "I'm sure you have more enemies than I do."

"Nope," he said. "Just you."

She glared at him, but he was focused on the road again and probably missed it. "I highly doubt that." He had to have made a lot of arrests in his years as a vice cop. "Luther could have ordered a hit on you."

"I'm sure he wouldn't be upset if I got hit in the cross fire," Clint agreed.

"Were you?" she asked. "You need to pull over, so I can look at your shoulder."

He glanced down at it as if he hadn't realized he was bleeding. "We're almost there."

"Where?" she asked. "Where are you taking me?"

"To the Payne Protection Agency," he said.

She shook her head. "I don't want a bodyguard," she said.

"You need one."

After the shooting, she really couldn't argue with him, especially if the officer really had been one of the people shooting at her. But there was one thing she could refuse. "I don't want you."

I don't want you.

Clint wasn't surprised. He knew she hated him—that she blamed him for her brother's death. She wasn't the only one who held him responsible. He did, too.

I don't want you.

Those words hung in the air between them in the SUV. She didn't want him, but he wanted her. He had since the first moment he'd seen her. She was beautiful in a way that went deeper than her golden skin. But even back then, when they'd first met, she hadn't liked him. She'd known—before Javier died—that working with Clint would get him killed.

Regret and remorse hung heavy on his shoulders, hurting more than the wound he hadn't noticed until she'd mentioned it. He was surprised she wanted to check it. But true to her word, once he pulled the SUV into the parking lot of Payne Protection, she was reaching over the console.

But when she peeled away the edges of the torn jacket and shirt, he flinched, and a curse slipped out between his gritted teeth. "Pouring salt in it?" he asked.

Her full lips curved slightly. "Unfortunately, I don't have any with me."

She touched it again, and pain radiated down his arm. He asked, "Are you sure?"

"I didn't have time to grab the shaker before you tossed me out the window," she reminded him. "The blood is starting to clot. But you're going to need some stitches so you don't have a jagged scar. And some antibiotics. You must have hit it on the edge of the dumpster, because I don't see a bullet."

"Bullet probably would have hurt less." The minute the words left his lips, he regretted it—especially when he saw the smile slide away from her lips, turning them down into a grimace.

She pulled her hand away from his shoulder. "Javier probably wouldn't agree with you—if he had survived."

"I'm sorry," he murmured. But he knew the apology, which he'd uttered many times, would never be enough for her. It wouldn't bring back her little brother, and that was the only way she would ever forgive him.

But even if he couldn't gain her forgiveness, he needed her trust. "We're here," he said, and gestured toward the building. Lights glowed through the windows in the brick walls.

She glanced at the building. "Good." When she reached for the door handle, Clint caught her shoulder to hold her back.

"You can't get out yet."

She turned toward him with her dark eyes narrowed. "You can't keep me—"

He already knew that. "I have to make sure it's safe," he explained.

"Nobody could have followed us here," she said, "not with the crazy way you were driving."

He glanced around the parking lot, which was brightly lit with streetlamps. "Not followed," he agreed. "But they could be here."

"How?"

"You don't think any of Luther's shooters would recognize me?" he asked. He'd worked vice so long that most of them had to know who he was. "You don't think Luther knows where I work now?"

She shivered as she looked out the windows, too. "Then you shouldn't have brought me here, either."

He sighed because he couldn't argue with her. "I probably shouldn't have. But the chief is here. He wants to talk to all of you."

"The chief?"

"Police Chief Woodrow Lynch."

"The former FBI guy." She shivered again.

Lynch was intimidating, which was probably one reason why Parker hadn't refused the assignment. Another was that Parker felt like Clint did—like they all did—about Luther Mills. He had to be stopped.

"And who is all of us?"

"Everybody Luther threatened in those phone calls. The CSI tech, the prosecutor, the judge's daughter, the arresting officer…" All of Luther's victims in one place.

It had been stupid to bring her here, to bring any of them here. A wave of nausea washed over him at the thought that he might have put her in more danger.

"Are you okay?" Rosie asked as she turned fully toward him again. She reached out and pressed her hand to his face.

Clint braced himself, but her touch affected him,

making his pulse quicken and his breath catch in his lungs.

"You're really warm," she said. "Have you had a tetanus shot lately? You could be getting an infection from the metal that cut your shoulder."

He was getting hot, but that was more from her touch than anything else. Her hand was cool against his face, but her soft skin made his tingle.

"When was your last tetanus shot?" she persisted.

From Javier singing her praises and from what Clint himself heard around the hospital about her, he already knew that she was a good nurse. But now he knew how good, that she could put aside her hatred of him for concern for his health.

He shook his head. "I don't know."

"We need to get you to the ER," she said. "You need stitches and a tetanus shot."

"I'm fine," he said.

He wasn't worried about himself. He was worried about her, that he might have put her in more danger by bringing her here. He'd made a promise to her brother, and this one he would not break.

But when he noticed shadows near the building, he realized that the choice might not be left up to him. There were people out there moving within those shadows.

He had made damn certain the shooters from her apartment hadn't followed them. But they wouldn't have had to follow them. They could have followed any one of the other bodyguards back here from collecting the person he or she had been assigned to protect.

Other Payne Protection SUVs were already parked in the lot.

Luther hadn't ordered a hit on everyone for tonight. Just Rosie.

But Luther was such a control freak that he would probably have some of his people watching his other potential victims, so he would know where they were when he was ready to take them out. And if Luther had learned the Payne Protection Agency was guarding them, he could have figured out where they would all meet up.

And if he had figured it out, he had to be laughing his ass off that they'd made it so easy for him to take out all his victims in one place.

Maybe he was just being paranoid and giving Luther way too much credit. But he knew the drug dealer too well to ever underestimate him again. Luther Mills was always at least one step ahead of everyone else. Usually more. That was how he had avoided prosecution for so many years.

No. Clint would not make the mistake of underestimating him ever again. The last time he had, someone had died. Rosie's brother.

A curse slipped out, and Clint reached for the keys still dangling from the ignition.

"What?" Rosie asked, her eyes widening with fear. "What's wrong?"

Just as Clint started up the SUV again, those shadows moved away from the building toward his vehicle. He could drive over one or two of them—but not all of them.

Ignoring the pain in his shoulder, he reached for his

weapon as he pushed Rosie below the windows. "Get down!" he told her.

He would do his best to protect her. But the guilt that always weighed on his shoulders now reminded him that his best had not been good enough for Javier.

Chapter 3

"**P**ut down the gun!" Parker shouted as he pulled open the driver's door of the SUV. He was not going to get shot in front of his own damn agency. And definitely not by a member of his team.

"Damn it!" Clint cursed him. "I nearly shot you. Why the hell were you all sneaking up on me?"

Parker was not alone. "You were sitting out here for a while," he said. And he and some of the other guards—ones he'd borrowed from his brothers' agencies to secure the perimeter during their meeting—had grown concerned. And maybe with good reason. "We thought something was wrong."

As Clint slid his weapon back into his holster, a grimace crossed his face with the movement. He was hurt.

"What the hell happened?" Parker asked.

Clint had warned him that he was the last man the

witness would want to protect her. Apparently, Parker should have listened to him.

The witness answered before Clint could. "He threw us out a third-story window," she said.

Maybe Clint was the one Parker should have been worried about. "What?" he asked.

She had to be lying, maybe trying to get her bodyguard in trouble.

"We were being shot at," Clint explained. "When you all started creeping up on us, I thought the shooters might have followed us here."

"Not with the way you were driving," the brunette remarked. From her disparaging tone, it was clear that Clint had not exaggerated how Rosie Mendez felt about him.

"Are you hurt?" Parker asked her.

She shook her head. "No. But he needs stitches and a tetanus shot." Despite her hostility toward her bodyguard, there was concern in her voice. There was also knowledge; the hospital badge dangling from the pocket of her scrubs identified her as a registered emergency medicine nurse.

"I'm fine," Clint said, but as he slid out from beneath the steering wheel, he flinched again. He was not fine. But he was clearly focused on protecting the witness regardless of his injury and her resentment of him. He pushed past Parker and the other bodyguards to open the passenger's door.

"You need to go to the hospital," she told him, and she stayed seated as if she intended to go with him.

"The chief of the River City Police Department is waiting to talk to you and the others," Parker said. And he felt a rush of pride that that man was his stepfather.

His mother had married a good man this time. "I'll have someone else take Clint to the ER."

"I'm not going anywhere," Clint stated albeit through gritted teeth. "I am fine. I can do my job."

Parker sighed. "I can't argue that—not after you saved her from getting shot and made sure you weren't followed getting here."

Yes. He had chosen his team well. Too well to lose any of them. And one of them was already hurt, no matter how damn fine he swore he was.

He'd known when he'd accepted this assignment from the chief that it would be dangerous. But he'd had no idea that the danger would start almost immediately.

Heat rushed to Rosie's face. She must have sounded ungrateful to the bodyguards who'd gathered around the SUV. Clint Quarters had saved her from getting shot, and instead of thanking him, all she'd done was complain.

But it was easier for Rosie to complain about Clint than to be grateful to him. She just couldn't do it.

Not after what he'd cost her. And no matter how many times he might save her life, he could never bring back the life lost because of him.

Javier...

She had no intention of going along with his being her bodyguard. That was the reason she walked into the Payne Protection Agency with him and the others. She intended to tell the chief of police exactly what he could do with his protection.

Not that she could deny that she needed it. What had happened to that young officer who'd escorted her home? Had Luther really gotten to him? Either paying or threatening him? Or had the shooters taken him out first before Clint came to her rescue?

And he had rescued her. But that didn't mean he had to be the one to protect her until she testified. It looked as though the Payne Protection Agency had many other bodyguards. Several patrolled the parking lot and the outside of the brick building while many more stood inside the doors.

She should have felt safe seeing all those armed and trained bodyguards. But the danger became even more real than when those shots had rung out. That had been so surreal and Clint had reacted so quickly that she was almost able to believe that it hadn't happened at all.

But then he stepped around her, and she could see his shoulder in the bright interior light. His jacket and shirt were torn and so was his skin, the edges of the wound ragged and oozing blood yet.

It had definitely happened. They had come under attack and nearly been killed.

"You really need medical attention," she persisted.

He shrugged off her concern. "I'm fine."

"You're stubborn," she said with frustration, that he wouldn't listen to her. He might know about being a cop and a bodyguard. But she, as an ER nurse, knew about injuries like his.

It couldn't go untreated.

"You have no idea," another man murmured. It was the one who'd pulled open Clint's door. He was tall with dark hair and blue eyes. "I'm Parker Payne," he introduced himself.

And she realized he was the boss.

He led her toward another room, a conference room, and when that door opened, she saw who was really running the show. At least *this* show...

Chief Woodrow Lynch. She'd met him before. He'd come to Javier's funeral to express his condolences. Unlike Clint, he hadn't been thrown out. He'd seemed sincere and determined to make certain that her brother's killer was finally brought to justice.

"I'm so glad you're here, Ms. Mendez," he greeted her. "We were getting worried about you."

"You weren't the only one," she murmured.

"Clint thwarted an attempt on her life," Parker said.

Jocelyn Gerber, the assistant district attorney, jumped up from her chair. She was tall and thin with pin-straight black hair.

Rosie envied all of that—the height, the weight and the straight hair. Rosie wasn't much over five feet tall. And if not for her busy schedule at the hospital, she would probably be carrying more than a few extra pounds. And even a straightener couldn't get rid of her stubborn curls.

"Are you all right?" Ms. Gerber asked.

Rosie wasn't certain if the woman was concerned about her or just about her case against Luther Mills. The young ADA was blatantly ambitious.

Rosie nodded but turned back toward the chief. "What about your officer?" she asked. "The one you had protecting me?"

The chief looked over her head at Clint. "There was no one at her door when I arrived at her apartment," Clint informed him. "I'm not sure what happened to the officer."

"I'll find out," someone said before the chief could.

The detective who'd arrested Luther made the offer as he jumped up from his chair at the long conference table.

Rosie felt sick with concern that the officer could have been hurt because of her.

Like Clint had been hurt...

"You're not going anywhere," the chief told Detective Dubridge.

"But you heard them—there's been a shooting," he said. "I need to investigate."

"Someone else is taking that case. You're not the only detective with River City PD. But you are the only one with a hit out on you. You need to sit back down," the chief said, and his tone brooked no argument.

The detective must have sensed that as well because the tall, dark-haired man sat back down next to a small blonde woman.

The chief turned back to Rosie. "Please, take a seat as well," he directed her. He didn't wait for her to comply before he stepped back from the conference table, took his cell from his pocket and made a call.

Despite his injured shoulder, Clint pulled out a chair for her. Her knees shaking suddenly, she sank onto it and glanced around the long table.

Jocelyn Gerber and Detective Dubridge were not the only people Rosie recognized. Judge Holmes sat at the table, too. He looked a lot like the chief, with iron-gray hair and an expressionless face. She couldn't imagine anyone threatening that intimidating man. But then she remembered that Clint had said the person in danger was his daughter. She must have been the girl sitting between him and a burly bearded man. Despite the late hour, the young blonde looked as though she'd just stepped off the runway of a fashion show. In a sparkling evening gown, she was supermodel-status glamorous.

Which made Rosie feel tired and dirty in the scrubs she'd worn for a double shift. They hadn't been very clean even before she'd wound up in the dumpster.

At least one of the other women around the table was dressed as if she'd already been in bed for the night—and alone, as Rosie had intended to be. She wore loose yoga pants and an oversize T-shirt. Her short red hair was tousled around a face devoid of makeup—of any color at all but for a sprinkling of freckles across her nose and cheeks. She was still prettier than Rosie felt, though.

Not that she had anyone she wanted to impress. But for some reason, as that thought entered her mind, she glanced over at Clint, who'd taken the chair next to her. She wasn't concerned about his opinion of her. But unfortunately, she was concerned about him. His handsome face contorted with another grimace and it was clear to see he was in pain. That might have had something to do with his boss, who touched his shoulder.

"Are you sure there isn't a bullet in it?" Parker asked him.

"Bullet?" the woman in the pajamas asked, and there was something like eagerness in her voice. "Were you shot?"

"No," Clint replied. "So don't start trying to dig a bullet out of me for evidence."

Apparently, she was the evidence tech who'd been threatened.

So they were all here—all the people Luther Mills intended to kill. Maybe Rosie should have felt better knowing that she was not the only one. But she couldn't feel good about other people being in danger.

The chief clicked off his cell and stepped back to the table. His brow was furrowed, and it looked as though he had more lines in his face than she remembered him having.

"Is the officer..." Dead? She couldn't say it. Couldn't say that word. She'd already said it too many times.

The chief shook his head. "No. He's alive. But he had been knocked out."

"Really? He wasn't in the hall when I arrived," Clint said. "And he never should have left her door." He sounded suspicious. He seemed convinced that Luther had already gotten to the officer.

But he was so young, so like Javier, that Rosie didn't want to believe it. "Maybe he heard something and went to investigate," she said.

"The detective didn't say where he'd been found," the chief said.

Rosie didn't care. "Is he okay?" she asked. Concussions were serious.

She glanced back at Clint. Had he hit his head as well as his shoulder? She wanted to reach out and run her fingers through his soft-looking golden hair. But just to look for a bump or a cut—that was the only reason. She resisted the urge despite her fingers twitching. When she requested a different bodyguard, she would insist he go to the ER.

Realizing that the chief had hesitated a long time before answering her question, she turned back to him. "Is Officer Maynard okay?"

She remembered his name because he'd reminded

her of Javier. But she couldn't remember the names of all the other officers who'd guarded her since Javier's murder. There had been too many.

Chief Lynch nodded. "He'll be fine."

"Could he be the leak?" Detective Dubridge asked. He must have picked up on Clint's suspicion.

The chief shook his head. "He doesn't have access to everything that Luther found out about the upcoming trial. No one in the police department does."

The detective and the chief turned to the assistant district attorney. Jocelyn Gerber's pale face flushed. "You're saying there's a leak in my department?" She sounded deeply insulted.

"If the leak is there, why do we need a private security company?" The crime scene tech asked the question Rosie had opened her mouth to ask as well. "Why can't we just have officers protect us?"

"Because the officer at Rosie's was so effective?" Clint asked the question. "She had no protection when I arrived. She would have been killed for certain."

She shivered as she realized how true that was—with all those bullets flying, there was no way she would have survived. Despite all the locks on the door, they would have gotten inside her apartment—they would have gotten to her.

Luther Mills had no intention of letting her testify against him.

"I think the private security firm is a great idea," Jocelyn said. "Because I don't think the leak is in the DA's office. A higher-ranking police officer or a detective would be able to get information about the trial."

Dubridge glared at her. "Are you accusing me of helping out Luther Mills?"

"Not at all," she assured him. "But you're not the only detective with the River City PD."

"He just thinks he is," the blonde sitting next to him murmured.

Rosie felt like an extreme outsider in this meeting. All these people appeared to know one another much better than she knew any of them except Clint Quarters. And her animosity and resentment for him wasn't the only animosity and resentment in the room.

Jocelyn ignored the comments and continued, "I just think the witness is the only one we need to worry about protecting at the moment."

Detective Dubridge nodded in agreement of that. "She's right. The only assassination attempt was made on the witness."

The witness. That was all she was to them. Suddenly very cold, she shivered.

The chief shook his head. "You were all threatened," he said. "You will all have a bodyguard."

The room erupted with protests, everyone arguing. Even the judge. He argued with his daughter, who clearly didn't want a bodyguard either.

Detective Dubridge's deep voice was the loudest. "How the hell is Bodyguard Barbie going to protect me?" he asked disdainfully.

And the blonde sitting next to him bristled with anger over his chauvinism.

Rosie would have preferred the blonde to Clint Quarters. She would have preferred anyone to Clint Quarters. But she doubted her protests would be heard above all the others. So she stood up and turned toward the chief. "May I speak to you alone?"

"Ms. Mendez needs a bodyguard more than anyone else," Jocelyn Gerber said. "As the eyewitness to the murder, she needs to make it to trial."

That was all the prosecutor cared about, apparently—getting a conviction. Rosie cared about more than that; she wanted justice for her brother and she wanted Luther Mills to never be able to hurt anyone else. Being in jail wasn't preventing that, though.

Would being in prison? She hoped so.

"She's the only one who really needs protection," Detective Dubridge added. "The rest of us have lives to live, work to do."

"And I don't?" she asked, her temper snapping.

He'd been so nice to her when Javier had been shot. But maybe, like Jocelyn Gerber wanted that conviction, he'd only wanted that arrest. Getting Luther was all they seemed to care about.

But she had patients and a job she cared about as well. The hospital was short-staffed. If she didn't show up to work, people could die. Or she could lose her job. Then how would she support herself after the trial? How would she pay her rent and her bills?

The chief stepped forward and took her elbow. "Of course you may speak to me," he said as he escorted her from the noisy conference room. "But Parker Payne will join us."

She didn't care who joined them as long as it wasn't Clint Quarters. But he'd stood up when she had, as if he'd needed to shield her from bullets inside the protection agency. She grabbed the chief's arm. "Not him. I don't want him to join us."

Even though he had saved her life, she didn't want

Clint Quarters anywhere near her. Maybe it was partially *because* he had saved her life that she didn't want him near her. She didn't want her feelings for him to change out of gratitude. She wanted to keep hating him. She needed to keep hating him.

Clint was hurting like hell. And it wasn't just his shoulder. His entire body ached from hitting whatever the hell had been inside that dumpster. But he'd already been hurting, even before he'd jumped out that window.

Since Javier died, he'd been aching with guilt and regret and loss. He'd really cared about that kid. He couldn't imagine how badly Rosie hurt.

And he didn't want her to hurt anymore. He had to be the one to protect her.

"I need to be in that meeting, too," he said as he followed Parker, the chief and Rosie out into the hallway.

"No!" she protested sharply. "I don't want him."

That was no doubt what she was going to tell Parker and the chief. That would she would be okay with any other bodyguard but him.

He'd already warned Parker that was how she would feel, that she would not want him protecting her. But even if for some reason Parker took him off the case, he wouldn't stop guarding her.

He intended to keep at least that promise he'd made to Javier. He would make sure nothing happened to his sister, even if protecting her caused him more pain.

Even if it cost him his life.

But as he watched her walk away from him, looking so beautiful even as exhausted as she was, it wasn't just his life he was worried about.

He was worried about his heart, too. He could easily fall for Rosie and not just into a dumpster.

Chapter 4

Just before the door to Parker Payne's office closed, Rosie caught a glimpse of Clint Quarters's handsome face. And the look on it jolted her.

There was such an intensity in his deep green eyes. And something else, something she almost suspected was fear.

But she doubted Clint Quarters would care that he got removed from the assignment as her bodyguard. She couldn't imagine he would choose to protect her, not when he knew how much she hated him.

Maybe he was afraid that his boss wouldn't remove him and that he would be hurt even more than he'd already been. Rosie had that fear, too.

Parker Payne closed the door, though, and broke the contact between Rosie and Clint. She wished she could put him as easily from her mind. But she thought about him entirely too much. Javier had idolized the former vice cop. His idol had gotten him killed.

She blinked back the tears that stung her eyes at the thought of her brother's death. That was the only reason she thought about Clint Quarters too much—because she thought about Javier so often.

"Are you okay?" Chief Lynch asked, his deep voice warm with fatherly concern.

Not that she knew much about fathers. She couldn't remember hers. And Javier's hadn't stuck around for long, either, not that she could blame them with the mess her mother had been.

"Were you injured at all during that attempt on your life?" the chief asked.

"No," she said. "I'm fine."

But she wasn't. She was shaken, and not just because she'd been shot at. She was shaken because of Clint Quarters, because he'd been the one who'd saved her.

"Clint Quarters is the one who needs to go to the ER," she insisted.

Parker nodded his dark head in agreement. "I'll make sure he goes."

"So you'll give me another bodyguard?" she asked. Maybe it would be easier than she'd thought it would be to get rid of Clint.

Parker sighed. But before he could say anything, she spoke again.

"Actually I don't want any bodyguard," Rosie insisted. "I have a job." One that she loved. "I have to go to work. I can't put my life on hold for this trial."

The chief uttered a weary-sounding sigh. "You have

to," he told her, "if you want your brother's killer to be brought to justice."

Her eyes stung again, so she blinked harder. "Of course I want that. I have every intention of testifying against Luther Mills."

"You won't be able to if you're dead," Parker said.

She flinched at his brutal honesty.

"Parker," the chief admonished him. "You don't need to be so blunt."

"It's the truth," Parker said. "And she needs to hear it. She cannot refuse protection."

"Protection, fine," she agreed. "Just any bodyguard but Clint Quarters."

Parker sighed. "Clint said you wouldn't want him as your bodyguard."

He must have already tried to pass off the assignment to someone else. She felt a twinge at that, but it couldn't have been disappointment. She was relieved that he had, because it bolstered her argument against his being her bodyguard. "He knows I hate him."

"Why do you hate him?" the chief asked, his brow furrowed with confusion. "Clint Quarters was a highly decorated police officer with an exemplary record before Parker stole him from the force for his team."

She snorted. *Exemplary record.* She wouldn't call it that, not when a twenty-year-old had lost his life because of him. That should have put a hell of a black mark on his exemplary record.

"How do you even know each other?" the chief asked. "Did you have a personal relationship?"

Did he think she was a jilted lover or something?

"No!" she hotly denied. "He's the one who got my brother killed."

The chief shook his head. "I don't understand."

"Javier Mendez was Clint's informant on Luther Mills's organization," Parker explained to the chief.

"He forced him to become an informant," Rosie said. "He arrested my brother and planted drugs on him and threatened to have him sent to prison for years if he didn't help him get Luther Mills."

Parker's brow furrowed now. "Is that what your brother told you?" he asked. "Because there's no way in hell that Clint Quarters framed anyone for anything! He was one of the best damn officers I ever worked with."

"His record is exemplary." The chief repeated his earlier praise.

And Rosie's face heated as her temper boiled over. "My brother was no drug dealer!" Especially not for Luther Mills. She'd worked too hard to keep Javier away from him. "So Clint had to have framed him."

"Did your brother tell you that?" Parker persisted.

Rosie had to shake her head. "No. But he idolized Clint Quarters. He wouldn't have said a bad word about him."

"He wouldn't have idolized a man who framed him and forced him to do something he hadn't wanted to do," the chief said, and again his voice was all warm and fatherly.

Or at least what she figured a father probably sounded like. But she understood why her and Javier's fathers hadn't stuck around after getting their mom pregnant. Their mother, a drug addict, had been a difficult person to love. That was why Javier wouldn't have started selling drugs for anyone—least of all Luther.

He wouldn't have wanted to help anyone become what their mother had. He wouldn't have.

She blinked hard again, fighting against a new rush of tears.

"You know the truth," Parker told her, but more gently now, his voice almost sounding fatherly as well. "About your brother and about Clint. You just can't face it."

"No…" she murmured.

"And you know no one else will protect you like Clint will," Parker continued. "He feels guilty as hell over what happened to Javier. That's why he quit the force and finally joined my team."

"Is that why?" the chief asked. "I would have thought he'd want that arrest for himself."

Parker stared at Rosie as he replied, "If arresting Mills was all he cared about, he definitely would have."

Her head felt light, making her dizzy as she realized that Parker was right, maybe about everything. But that wasn't possible.

That could *not* be possible.

He was off the assignment. Clint knew it even before the door opened to Parker's private office. He'd warned his boss. There was no way Rosie would let him protect her. So if she'd given them an ultimatum—no protection or another bodyguard—they would have had to choose to assign her another bodyguard.

They had no choice, really.

It was clear from how Jocelyn Gerber had acted that her case, and a conviction of Luther Mills, hinged on Rosie's eyewitness testimony. Without it and her, the killer would walk to kill again.

Clint didn't want that any more than the others did. But he didn't believe any other bodyguard in that room would protect Rosie like he would. Sure, they were all good.

Even Bodyguard Barbie, as Spencer Dubridge had dubbed Keeli Abbott, was damn good. She'd held her own in the vice unit. She was far tougher than she looked. But none of the other bodyguards had the incentive Clint had to make sure Rosie stayed safe.

They hadn't made a promise to her brother like he had.

That was his only incentive.

It wasn't because he had personal feelings for Rosie. Hell, if he did—if he really did—that might prove more a hindrance than a help. A distraction and a detriment over an incentive.

No. He did not. He could not have feelings for Rosie Mendez. Sure, she was beautiful—inside and out. And strong and brave and smart.

But she was also stubborn and hateful and...

The door opened, and she stepped out into the hall. And all his negative thoughts left as he gasped again at her beauty. Even the dark circles beneath her big brown eyes didn't detract from her appearance. She was exhausted but beautiful.

Maybe that exhaustion was why Parker told him, "Take her to the safe house now."

She must have been too tired to fight hard enough to get him fired. That wasn't like her. She was so strong, such a fighter.

And now he looked at her with concern. When he'd jumped out that window with her in his arms, he'd been careful so that he would take the brunt of the fall. And his throbbing shoulder attested to the fact that he had.

But had she been hurt as well? Despite his efforts?

"Are you okay?" he asked her.

She nodded, but she didn't look at him. Then she brushed past him as she headed toward the exit. Clearly, she was ready to leave.

She definitely had to be exhausted.

But before Clint could head out with her, Parker caught his arm.

He suppressed a wince as the movement jarred his injured shoulder and turned toward his boss.

"Are you sure you're up to this?" Parker asked.

And Clint knew the other man wasn't talking about his shoulder. He was talking about Rosie.

No doubt she'd made it very clear to him, and to the chief who was studying him as well, how much she hated Clint. They confirmed this when Parker said, "Luther Mills might not be the only one you're in danger from."

If Rosie really wanted him dead, she would have killed him when he'd shown up for Javier's funeral. And she certainly wouldn't have been as concerned as she'd been in the SUV about his injury. No, Rosie Mendez was no killer.

And Clint had to make certain she didn't become the next victim of one.

"I'm fine," he assured his boss and the chief. "I've got this."

But because she'd already made it across the lobby to the front doors, he had to rush after her. Not that any of the perimeter guards would have let her step outside without protection.

Hell, they followed both of them to the SUV. While he opened the passenger door for her, one of Cooper Payne's team had already opened the driver's door and checked inside and underneath the vehicle. Cooper's guys were all highly trained former Marines.

They knew to check for explosives and other potential deadly threats. Luther Mills was probably quite a bit like the terrorists they'd faced on their missions. Crazy and determined with no conscience.

So it was good the former Marines were his backup. But as soon as he closed the driver's door, Rosie turned toward him and asked, "Can you lose them?"

"Who?" He glanced around the lot. Had someone followed him or the others? Was the area not as secure as he thought?

"Those guards," she said. "They're going to follow us, right?"

Given how everyone had been the most concerned about her—and after the shooting attempt, with good reason—Clint had no doubt the Marines were his reinforcements. "Probably."

"Then can you lose them?" she asked.

"If I wanted to," he said, and he wasn't trying to impress her, he was just stating a fact when he added, "I could." But he didn't want to. He wasn't exactly a hundred percent after diving out that window into the dumpster.

"If you really want to protect me, you need to," she advised him.

"Why?" he asked as he started the SUV and shifted into drive. "Don't you trust them?"

Had she recognized one of them from Luther's crew? Clint didn't know any of the ex-Marines very well. He didn't even know if they were from River City or not. They could have once worked for Luther. Pretty much everyone in her neighborhood had except for Rosie.

Luther didn't give his workers any choice. Just like he hadn't given Javier a choice.

But the young man had made one of his own. He'd chosen to stop the dangerous drug dealer. But that choice had cost him his life.

"I don't trust you," she said.

He flinched even though this wasn't news to him. Of course she didn't trust him, not after what had happened to her brother.

"I'm going to keep you safe," he promised as he drove the SUV out of the parking lot of the Payne Protection Agency.

"How?" she asked. "If that shoulder wound doesn't get treated, you're going to develop an infection or you'll just eventually bleed out. You need medical attention."

She was probably right—after all, she was the one with the medical experience. And Clint couldn't deny that he felt like hell.

But he shook his head. "I need to take you to the safe house first." Just like Parker had ordered. "Then I'll go once I know you'll be okay."

"You'll spend hours waiting to get seen at the ER," she said. "Unless I go with you."

He narrowed his eyes and glanced across at her face. Was she up to something? Did she intend to shake off his protection at the hospital?

She wouldn't lose him as easily as Clint had lost those shooters, as easily as he could lose the Marines if he chose to. "Why can't they come along?" he asked with a jerk of his head toward the SUV following them.

"Because I don't want everyone at the hospital to know that I'm in danger," she said.

"Don't they know about the trial?" he asked. "That you're going to testify against your brother's killer?"

"No," she said. "I haven't told anyone."

That had probably been a damn good idea, given that anyone could be affiliated with Luther and his crew. Rosie hadn't survived growing up in her neighborhood by luck. She was street-smart.

But as smart as she'd been to keep everything to herself, it must have been lonely as well. Had she had no one to support her through the loss of her brother?

"You didn't tell anyone?" he asked. "Not a friend? Or a boyfriend?"

She snorted. "With the hours I work I barely have time to sleep, let alone have a relationship of any kind."

So she needed the people she worked with to be her friends, like Clint felt the people he worked with were his. But unlike him, she felt like she couldn't trust her coworkers.

Clint glanced into his rearview mirror, at the lights shining in it. Parker would give him hell if he purposely lost his backup.

But Rosie was right. If she walked in with an entourage, everyone would know that something was wrong, that she was in danger. But even if she walked in with him...

"How are you going to explain me?" he asked.

Her eyes widened as she stared at him. "I hadn't thought about it."

"Guess you'll have to claim I'm your boyfriend," he told her.

A gasp slipped through her lips, and he didn't think it was because he suddenly jerked the wheel to the right. The tires squealed at the sharp turn.

And Rosie's dark eyes widened even more. But she didn't protest claiming him as hers.

Clint glanced away from her to study the rearview mirror. The lights were gone. The driver of the Payne agency SUV that had been following them hadn't expected Clint's sharp and sudden turn, so he missed it.

Clint made a few more hairpin turns in the circuitous route he traveled to the hospital. He hadn't tried really hard to lose his tail, though—just to make it look as though he had to Rosie.

For some reason she hadn't forced Parker to remove him from this assignment. And for that reason, he didn't want to piss her off. So he would go along with what she wanted.

He just hoped like hell that complying with her wishes wouldn't get them both killed.

Luther stared down at the cell phone in his hand, willing it to ring. Where the hell was she? She couldn't have just disappeared, and his crew had looked all around her building for her body.

For hers and Clint Quarters's.

They were both gone.

Damn Quarters!

The former vice cop hadn't killed her when he'd tossed her out that window. He'd saved her. How the hell was that man so damn lucky?

How could they have fallen three stories and not been hurt? They had to be at the hospital. At least that was what Luther was counting on...

Chapter 5

"I didn't even know you were seeing anyone," Anita Cruz remarked as she rubbed her shoulder against Rosie's as they stood together at the nurses' station.

Despite her reluctance, Rosie had had to claim that Clint was her boyfriend in order to get him moved to the top of the long waiting list in the ER. Her coworkers often pulled favors like that, but she never had.

Until now.

Until Clint Quarters.

So it was only natural that everyone would be curious about him. About them.

But after getting shot at, she was a little paranoid. Maybe that was why she thought Anita sounded more suspicious than surprised. Anita, who was a little older than her, often called in favors for friends who Rosie suspected worked for Luther Mills—because their wounds were even more questionable-looking than Clint's.

She forced a smile. "It's pretty new," she said. "That's why I haven't mentioned it to anyone." Even if she had been seeing someone, she probably wouldn't have mentioned it to anyone, though.

She liked keeping work and her personal life separate. Not that she'd ever had much of a personal life.

Anita nodded. "Or do you just want to keep him all to yourself? He's pretty damn hot."

He was—especially as he sat, shirtless, on the stretcher just feet away from them in the emergency room. Golden hair covered some of the golden skin of his heavily muscled chest. His arms were heavy with muscles, too—his biceps bulging even though they weren't flexed.

Yes, he was pretty damn hot. That was the problem. Clint Quarters was too damn good-looking.

"So how'd he get hurt?" Anita persisted.

And goose bumps rose on Rosie's skin as a chill passed through her. Had Luther put out the word? Was he looking for her after she and Clint had escaped his gunmen? Was he that determined to finish the job?

The trial wasn't set to begin for a few weeks yet. But he'd been in a jail for a while already. Maybe he was getting impatient to get out. And if the eyewitness was dead, the district attorney's office might be forced to drop the charges against him.

Of course Jocelyn Gerber seemed so determined to nail him that she might persist in trying him even without Rosie. She hoped the prosecutor did, just in case Rosie didn't survive the next attempt Luther made on her life.

And she knew he would try again.

That was why she hadn't fought Parker Payne as hard as she should have to replace Clint as her bodyguard—because she hadn't been able to argue with his results. He had saved her life once already.

She had to trust that he would again. But trusting Clint Quarters...

She shivered.

"Was it that bad?" Anita asked. "I only got a quick glance at his shoulder." Before she'd come out of the exam area to interrogate Rosie.

Clint was still visible from the nurse's station, though, since he'd pulled back the curtain the young resident had tried to pull around him. He hadn't done it so that she could see him, though. He'd done it so that he could see her. Even though he hadn't been a bodyguard very long, he obviously took his new job very seriously.

Rosie shook her head. "He—uh—wiped out on his motorcycle."

Anita peered across at Clint. "Doesn't look like road rash."

"Oh, he didn't fall," Rosie said.

No. He had jumped—and taken her along with him. But she'd escaped unscathed, thanks to him.

She continued, "He banged into something." Like a dumpster...or whatever had been inside it.

"Were you with him?" Anita asked with what sounded like genuine concern.

Guilt flashed through Rosie that she'd doubted the woman. She also regretted having to lie to her. "No. He was alone. Driving too fast."

"He doesn't seem like the careless type," Anita said. "He seems really intense." And now she shivered.

He wasn't just watching Rosie; he was staring at her coworker as well. Anita's curiosity must have made him suspicious, too.

Rosie lifted her hand and waved at him while forcing a smile. She wanted him to know he was overreacting. Anita was just nosy.

He lifted his hand, waving her over to him.

Anita released a lustful sigh. "I wish he was waving me over to him. That is one fine-looking man, Rosie. You done good, girl."

But Rosie hesitated before stepping away from the nurses' station. She felt safe there; she didn't feel safe with Clint, and it wasn't because of Luther Mills's threat.

Anita bumped her shoulder again. "Don't keep him waiting, honey. Someone else might scoop him up."

Did he have a girlfriend?

Javier had told her that he didn't, but how much had her brother really known about his idol? Obviously not that he would get him killed someday.

Or had he known?

Even before he'd been shot, Javier had said some things to her—things that had made her think he might have been concerned. But more about her than himself…

Her brother had been such a sweetheart.

Clint Quarters was not. He waved at her again, beckoning her to come to him. He probably would have come to her if he'd been able, but it looked as though the resident was stitching up his shoulder.

"He must want you to hold his hand," Anita remarked with a lustful grin. "I'm surprised you weren't by his side this whole time."

He had wanted her there, but Rosie had insisted he should have his privacy and she'd assured him that she wouldn't go far from him. He'd looked at her with even more suspicion than when he'd been staring at Anita. And she had no doubt that if she'd walked any farther away than the nurse's station, he would have come after her. Had he thought she'd convinced him to come here so that she could give him the slip?

Sure, she would rather not have him as her bodyguard. But after the shooting, she knew she needed one. Probably more than one. Maybe she shouldn't have had him lose the Payne Protection SUV that had been following them.

Before Clint could beckon for her again, she walked over to the stretcher on which he was sitting. The resident glanced over at her. "Where'd you find this guy, Rosie?"

"What—why?" she stammered. She hadn't found him; he had found her. Well, first he'd found Javier. While he'd taken her out of danger, he'd put her brother in it.

And no matter how damn good-looking he was, she couldn't forget or forgive that.

"He's some kind of superman," the young doctor remarked in awe. "He refused to take any kind of painkiller, just a local anesthetic. There's no way his shoulder is even numb yet, but he insisted I start stitching him up because he's in a hurry to get out of here."

"Can't you see why?" Clint asked him as he grinned at Rosie.

And her traitorous heart skipped a beat as her pulse began to race. Damn him for being so good-looking...

The resident's face flushed, and he stammered now. "Uh, yeah."

"So that looks good enough, Doc," Clint said, even though the resident was still suturing.

"You need a few more to close up the wound completely," the resident insisted.

But Clint was already pulling away.

"Let him finish," she told him through the smile she forced herself to hang on to.

"But sweetheart," Clint said, "we have plans, and we don't want to keep our friends waiting."

"Friends…" Who the hell was he talking about?

He was looking beyond her now. Had those other bodyguards followed them after all? She glanced behind her and noticed a couple of teenagers. They were definitely not Payne Protection bodyguards.

Why was Clint staring at them? Did he think they were some of Luther's crew?

He must have, because he used his free hand to tug her into the space with him. Then he told her, "Pull that curtain, honey."

The resident glanced nervously from one to the other of them. "Really, Mr. Quarters—"

"Clint." He corrected him as if he'd done it before. "And really, this is good enough." But he didn't wait for the young doctor to finish. Using his right hand, he grabbed the scissors from the suture tray and clipped off the thread and needle himself.

"And I don't suppose you want a prescription for painkillers?" the resident asked.

"No thanks," Clint told him.

The young doctor sighed and murmured. "Badass."

Why was it that Clint Quarters inspired such hero

worship in young men? What was it about him? That he was tough? That he was fearless?

But he wasn't really. She'd seen fear on his face right before she'd walked into that room with Parker Payne and the chief of police.

And she saw it now as he reached for his shirt. "We need to get out of here."

"Have fun," the resident said as he slipped away.

"What's wrong?" she asked.

"Those guys out there…"

"The teenagers?"

"They work for Luther."

"Are you sure?" she asked. "Or are you just being paranoid?" Like she'd been when Anita had questioned her.

"I'm being realistic," Clint said. "And it's time that you were, too. Did you really think Luther Mills would let you live to testify against him when he has never let anyone else?"

That was why he'd killed Javier—because her brother had been going to testify that Luther Mills was a major drug dealer.

Clint shook his head. "I'm surprised it took him this long to go after you."

She knew Luther had always had a thing for her, since they were kids in elementary school. Maybe that was why no one had ever hassled her growing up. But that had all changed now that he'd ordered the hit on her.

She glanced around the edge of the curtain. Neither of those teenagers looked hurt. They had no reason for being in the ER—except that they were probably looking for her.

"We need to get out of here," Clint said.

And this time she didn't argue with him. She knew she was in danger. And because of her, they had no backup.

Clint was glad he'd finally gotten through to Rosie. She took him the back way out of the ER, through the employees' locker room. Once inside the stark white-tiled room, he riffled in some of the open lockers, taking only the things that would aid in their escape.

"You can't do that!" she cried out in protest of his petty thefts as she glanced nervously at the door.

"I can guarantee that Luther sent more than a couple of teenagers out to look for you," he said. "We need to disguise ourselves in case more of his crew is waiting outside the hospital for you."

She opened her mouth, as if to argue some more. But he unbuttoned his jeans and dropped them.

And all she did was gasp.

It wasn't like he'd stripped down entirely in front of her. He wore boxers beneath his jeans. He stepped into the scrub pants and pulled them up, tying them low on his waist. They were too loose for him to tuck his weapon into the back of them, like he usually did with his jeans.

But he hadn't smuggled his Glock into the hospital that way. He'd carried it in a pocket of his leather bomber jacket. But in case any of the shooters from her apartment were here, he needed to change his look. He needed to ditch his torn jacket. He grabbed a white doctor's coat from another open locker and dropped his gun into the deep pocket of that before pulling it over the scrub shirt he already wore. A nurse, not Rosie, had had to cut off his torn and bloodied T-shirt.

"You can't—" she began again in protest.

"I have to," he interrupted.

Then he found her a parka with a fur-trimmed hood. Before they opened the back door that led out to the parking lot, he pulled the hood over her head. While he kept one hand in the deep pocket of that white jacket, wrapped around his weapon, he slid his other arm around her shoulders and pulled her close to his side.

She tensed against him and whispered, "What the hell are you doing?"

"My job," he said. But he might have been enjoying her closeness a little too much. She smelled good— like vanilla and some other spice.

"What?" she asked, her voice cracking with fear as she peered around them. "Do you see someone out here?"

The employee parking lot was dimly lit, so Clint couldn't see much. "No," he admitted. "But that doesn't mean they're not out here, watching us."

She looked up into his face, and her dark eyes were narrowed.

"If they're looking for you," he said, and he sincerely believed that they had been, "they're going to be checking out the employee parking lot."

She tried to wriggle out from beneath his arm. "But until we see someone, we don't need to act like..."

"Like lovers," he finished for her.

And she shuddered, probably in revulsion.

He would have laughed at her overreaction if it hadn't depressed him. No matter how much he tried, he would never be able to get her to stop hating him.

"Nobody working for Luther will think it's us walking

through the lot if we're acting like lovers," he explained to her. "Everybody knows how much you hate me."

Most of all him.

Maybe she'd taken that as a challenge, because she suddenly slid her arm around his waist and snuggled against his side. He tensed now, but not with revulsion. He tensed because his body was reacting to the closeness of hers.

She lifted her face to his and fluttered her lashes. "You're right," she said. "Everybody knows how much I hate you. They would never believe I'd be doing this..." Then she reached out and ran her fingertips along his jaw as she leaned even closer to him.

Now she was challenging him. And Clint had never turned away from a challenge before. He leaned down and brushed his mouth across hers.

She gasped in reaction.

And he deepened the kiss, pressing his lips against her silky soft ones. He nipped and nibbled at the fullness before sliding his tongue inside her mouth. She tasted so damn sweet, like that vanilla he smelled on her, and she was so hot.

His body tensed even more as desire gripped him. He wanted her, but the only thing he should want was to protect her. With passion overwhelming him, he was too distracted—too unaware of what and who might be around them.

His brilliant plan to elude Luther's crew had backfired. Instead of putting her in less danger, he'd put her and himself in more.

And not just in danger of being attacked.

He was in danger of wanting what he could never have: Rosie Mendez.

* * *

Parker cursed and barked into the phone. "How the hell did you lose him?"

"I didn't know he was going to try to shake us," the other man replied. "I thought he was probably taking a different route to the safe house."

"But he's not there," Parker surmised.

"He hasn't shown up yet."

Where the hell could he have gone? He'd refused to go to the ER. And there was no way in hell he would have taken the witness back to her place, not after the two of them had nearly been killed at her apartment.

It must have been that close call and Clint saving her from getting shot that had had Ms. Mendez changing her mind about his being her bodyguard. And Parker had thought he'd gotten through to her as well. But maybe he hadn't…

Maybe she had only agreed to have Clint as her bodyguard because she'd intended to ditch him and the security detail altogether the minute she had the chance.

Had she escaped Clint?

"Damn it," Parker murmured.

He couldn't have failed already in the assignment his stepfather had asked him to do. He couldn't have lost the eyewitness who would have finally put Luther Mills behind bars for the rest of his miserable life.

Chapter 6

Rosie's lips tingled from the contact with Clint's. His kiss had scattered her senses so much that she didn't even remember getting into the SUV. She didn't remember the drive to the safe house. She didn't remember anything but his mouth moving hungrily over hers.

Had that kiss just been part of his disguise to get past Luther's crew? Had those teenagers really been working for Luther, though?

She had no idea.

She couldn't think even now…of anything but that amazing kiss. Like she'd told Clint when he'd asked if she had any friends or a boyfriend, she didn't have time. Maybe that was why his kiss had affected her so much. It had been a long time since she'd had a date.

Not that she and Clint were dating.

He was just her bodyguard.

And that was the only way he was acting now, as he

helped her from the SUV, keeping his body between her and the street. If anyone shot at her, he would take the bullet.

And she had no doubt that he would willingly do that. She hadn't been able to argue that with Parker Payne. She hadn't been able to argue at all when he'd said what he had about Javier.

Her brother wouldn't have kept apologizing to her if he'd done nothing wrong, if Clint had framed him. But even then she hadn't been able to deal with the knowledge of what Javier had done.

Of how she'd failed to keep him away from Luther.

She couldn't deal with any of that right now—with the truth or the guilt. And she certainly couldn't deal with the way that Clint's kiss had made her feel.

How could she have reacted that way to him? She should have been repulsed. No matter how much truth there might have been to what Parker Payne had said, she still blamed the former vice cop for her brother's death.

It was still Clint's fault. His and Luther Mills's.

Luther wanted her dead now.

And Clint…

What did her bodyguard want?

Her?

It had felt like that when he'd kissed her. He'd kissed her so passionately, so hungrily…

Rosie couldn't remember ever being kissed like that, with such need. It hadn't been just part of the act, of his lovers' disguise. Had it?

She glanced up at him, but he wasn't looking at her. He was peering around the street, probably looking for more of Luther's crew. But the only people present were the bodyguards from Payne Protection.

"You better call Parker," one of them advised him. "He's pissed."

That was her fault for making Clint lose them before going to the hospital. But she had been right, hadn't she? Anita and the others would have been even more suspicious had she shown up with the whole protection team. Then if Luther's crew had been at the hospital, there would have been some kind of altercation. Maybe another shooting.

Could she go back to the ER? She wanted to keep working, wanted to keep as much of her life as normal as possible. She'd already lost too much.

And to keep her life as normal as possible, she had to keep hating Clint Quarters.

Hating, not wanting, not kissing…

He pressed the buttons on a control panel in the wall of an old warehouse, and a steel door opened. "In here," he told her, touching the small of her back to guide her inside.

Even through the parka and her scrubs, she could feel the imprint of his hand. She wanted it on her skin, wanted it moving over her body. Despite her best efforts to hang on to that hatred for him, his kiss had awakened something inside her. Something she had ignored for far too long. And now it—that desire— refused to be ignored.

She shivered.

"Nobody's used the place for a while," he said. "So the heat probably needs to be turned up." He moved to a control panel on the inside, pushing buttons that slid the door closed again and had the furnace kicking in with a deep rumble. "It'll warm up fast."

She doubted that. The ceiling was high, open rafters, the walls brick and the floors hardwood. It was a nice apartment, but there was nothing warm about it.

He gestured to a doorway off the open living area. "The master suite is through there. If you want to shower and change, there are always different sizes of clothing stocked in the closet."

"Payne Protection thinks of everything," she murmured. She only wished she had as well, before she'd played along with his little charade in the parking lot. She'd only intended to disarm him when she'd acted all flirty. She hadn't thought he would take the charade even further with that kiss.

He nodded. "Yes, they do."

"I would prefer to have my own clothes," she said. Not that she had ever been able to afford much, but she would be more comfortable in her own stuff.

"We can send someone to your apartment to pack up some of your things," he offered.

She shook her head, rejecting the idea of strangers riffling through her belongings. "I want to go myself," she said.

He snorted. "Are you crazy? You nearly got killed there. You can't go back there."

"I can't stay here until the trial," she said. "I can't put my life and my job on hold for weeks."

"You have to," he said, "if you're going to stay alive to make it to the trial. You saw those kids at the hospital. They were looking for you."

She shook her head. "You don't know that. You're just trying to scare me."

"I'm not the one who shot at you," he said.

"No, you're the one who threw me out a window." To save her life…

She knew that was why he'd done it, but she couldn't let it go. She couldn't be grateful to him. She needed to stay mad at him. She needed to hate him or she might just start needing him.

And that scared her even more than having men shooting at her.

Clint flinched as the bedroom door shut behind Rosie. She hadn't slammed it. And he wasn't in pain, at least not much. He flinched because he knew she was going to take a shower. She was going to change, and he would be imagining her naked, standing under a spray of water, droplets glistening on her golden skin.

He groaned now.

"You should have taken that prescription for pain-killers," she said through the door. She had heard his groan.

Heat rushed to his face. It was already everywhere else in his body. He'd been burning up since he'd kissed her.

That had been one hell of a mistake. He could taste her still on his lips, on his tongue…

Kissing her had definitely been a mistake. But it was one he wanted to repeat over and over again. First he had to deal with the other mistake he'd made. He drew his cell phone from his pocket. The screen was shattered, the phone blank. He must have broken it when he'd fallen in the dumpster, which probably explained why Parker hadn't been blowing up his phone since he'd purposely ditched the other Payne Protection SUV.

Because the Payne Protection Agency did think of everything, just like Rosie had said, it was also stocked with extra cell phones. He picked up one from the granite counter, and sure enough, it was already programmed with Parker's number. He tapped the contact and called him.

"It's me," he said when his boss answered.

"Where the hell have you been?" Parker demanded to know.

"At the ER."

"Are you okay? Is she?" Parker anxiously asked.

Clint sighed as he felt a twinge of guilt. He hadn't meant to worry his old friend. "Yeah, yeah, we're fine. She just insisted that I get stitched up."

No matter how much she hated him, she hadn't wanted him to bleed out or get infected. How much did she really hate him? She hadn't pushed him away when he'd kissed her.

For a moment he'd actually thought her lips had moved beneath his. And her tongue had brushed across his. But had that all just been part of the act?

He hadn't been acting, though.

"Why the hell did you purposely shake your backup?" Parker asked.

"She didn't want them all at the hospital," Clint said. "None of her coworkers know about the trial."

Parker snorted. "You believe that?"

"No." But Clint didn't think she'd lied to him.

It was just that River City, despite being nearly as big as Detroit, was still small-town in some areas, like the one Luther Mills had ruled before his arrest. Hell, he still ruled it even from jail, and the hospital where Rosie worked was within that area.

There was no way her coworkers weren't aware of what had happened to her brother and that she'd witnessed it. Rosie was just fooling herself about it, like she had so many other things.

He hadn't forced Javier to become an informant. Her brother had wanted to do it—for her. But Clint wouldn't tell her that. He would rather carry all the guilt himself than share any with her. She was already in enough pain over her brother's death. And now she might even lose her life, too.

"She wants to go back to the hospital," Clint warned his boss.

"You said she's not hurt."

"She wants to work," Clint said.

She wanted to pretend that she wasn't in danger, that nothing had changed. But she was fooling herself about that, too.

"She can't," Parker said. "She'll get herself killed and probably you, too."

Clint must have already made it clear to Parker that he wasn't going to quit the assignment no matter what. Maybe that was what his boss had told Rosie that had convinced her to agree to Clint's being her bodyguard.

Even a restraining order wouldn't have gotten him to stay away from her now that he knew how much danger she was in. But was he the right person to protect her?

He'd allowed himself to get distracted in the parking lot. He'd allowed her to distract him.

And even now, hearing the shower running, he could barely focus on his conversation with Parker. He couldn't think of anything but Rosie, standing naked under the water…

Another groan slipped out.

"I thought you went to the hospital," Parker said. "What did they do?"

"Stitched me up," he said.

"Didn't they give you painkillers?"

"I can't take any now," Clint said. He needed to stay alert to any potential threat.

But Rosie was more of a threat to his focus than the painkillers probably would have been.

"You're in the safe house," Parker said. The others must have reported his arrival. "So you have backup in place. You can get some rest."

That was easier said than done with Rosie so close to him, so naked...

"I'm fine," Clint assured his boss. If only he could convince himself.

"Get some rest," Parker repeated. "You're going to need it to deal with her."

Now the heat in Clint's body was anger. "What are you talking about? Sure, she's stubborn, but she—"

"Hates your guts," Parker said. "You have to keep one eye open for Luther Mills's crew and the other for her."

Clint couldn't argue with that. Rosie had wished him dead before. But if she was going to kill him, she would have done it that day he'd shown up for her brother's funeral. And she certainly wouldn't have insisted he get treatment for his shoulder wound if she'd wanted him dead.

"I'll be fine," Clint told him.

But his boss cursed and said, "I probably should have given her another bodyguard like she wanted."

"Why didn't you?" Clint asked. He'd really thought

Parker would try to take him off the assignment—per Rosie's demand.

"Because I know no one will work harder than you will to protect her."

Did he know why?

Clint hadn't mentioned his promise to Javier to anyone else. But the Payne family was notorious for their ability to just *know* things.

"No one will," Clint promised. "Thanks for not replacing me."

"Don't thank me," Parker told him. "I don't think I did the right thing."

"Why not?" They'd both just agreed that nobody would try harder to protect her.

Parker uttered a ragged sigh that rattled the cell phone. "Because I think this damn assignment will probably wind up getting you killed."

Clint wanted to argue with his boss, yet he couldn't. He would gladly give up his life for Rosie's. And he had a feeling that it just might come down to that before his assignment was over.

Luther Mills had never before let a witness live to testify against him.

The Payne Protection Agency.

Luther had heard of it. A person couldn't live in River City and not know about it. But he didn't just know the agency. He knew Parker Payne.

He leaned back on his bunk and chuckled. Parker Payne had tried for years to take him down. Instead, the former vice cop had nearly been taken down.

Too bad Parker hadn't died when that hit had been

put out on him years ago. So many assassins had tried…and failed. Regrettably.

Maybe Luther should put out another hit on Parker Payne and on every damn bodyguard working for him.

Luther knew all of them. Clint. Hart Fisher. Landon Myers and that little hottie, Keeli Abbott. They were all former vice cops who, like Parker and Clint Quarters, had tried for many years to take down Luther and his organization. But eventually, they'd all given up and quit the River City PD.

Luther ran his fingers over the cell phone that was still warm from his last, long conversation. He'd been apprised of the situation.

The chief knew that Luther had gotten to someone in the police department. Obviously, he didn't know who yet, or Luther wouldn't have gotten all the information he just had—that the chief had hired the Payne Protection Agency to guard the witness and everyone else associated with the case against him.

Someday soon, when he was free, he would have to thank Chief Lynch for making it all so easy for him. Now he wouldn't just take out the witness and the other people going after him, he would take out all those former vice cops as well.

He would take down everyone who had tried to take him down for so many years. But it wouldn't take him years to accomplish his objective.

Just days.

Or hours.

And all of them would be dead.

Chapter 7

Rosie had never felt so on edge with her nerves so frayed. It probably didn't help that she hadn't slept at all the night before. She wanted to blame that on getting shot at, but she knew the real reason: Clint Quarters.

She wished she'd been sleeping and that she had just dreamed that kiss and it had never actually happened. She felt like a traitor to herself—and to Javier.

No matter what he'd said at the end.

She shouldn't have let Clint Quarters kiss her—even if it had been just to fool whoever Luther might have sent to look for her. She should have shoved Clint away; instead, she'd...

Kissed him back. And she'd wanted to go on kissing him. That was why she'd lain awake the night before, her lips tingling, her body hot despite the cool shower she'd taken.

She'd wanted to kiss him again.

So she'd locked herself in that master bedroom, and she hadn't come out again until morning. She wasn't sure where he'd slept or if he'd slept at all. There were dark circles beneath his deep green eyes. The darker gold shadow of his beard was thicker now. He hadn't shaved. But he'd changed out of the scrubs into jeans and a long-sleeved black shirt.

Heat flashed through her as she remembered him dropping his jeans to change into the scrub pants. He'd worn boxers beneath but the material was knit and had left little to her imagination.

So that she'd been able to tell how tight his ass was, how muscular his thighs and his...

She mentally slapped herself. She needed to snap out of it. She was not attracted to Clint Quarters. Of course, when Javier had first introduced them, she'd thought he was handsome and nice and smart...until she'd discovered what he'd done, that he'd turned Javier into an informant against the most dangerous criminal in River City.

And there had been some very dangerous criminals in River City over the years. Most of them are off the streets now, and if the rumors she'd heard were true, the Payne Protection Agency was responsible for those arrests or deaths.

"Coffee?" Clint asked as he held up a pot he must have just brewed. The rich aroma floated across the granite kitchen counter into the open living room.

"Yes, please," she murmured, but she hesitated before approaching him. She didn't trust herself to get too close to him. But then years of training had her asking, "How is your shoulder?"

He grunted.

"You should have taken the prescription for pain-killers," she admonished him. He hadn't had to play superhero for her. Again. He'd already been her superhero when he'd saved her from the shooters at her apartment.

"We didn't have time to fill any prescriptions," he said as he walked around the counter. He held two cups of coffee. One he kept; the other he held out to her.

As she reached for it, her hand trembled slightly. Then her fingers brushed across his, making her skin tingle, and she shook so much she nearly sloshed the hot brew over the rim.

"Careful," he said as he steadied her hand on the cup.

But that only made her tremble more. Her blood heated from his touch.

"Do you need cream?" he asked. "Milk?"

She shook her head. She needed him. No. She needed to not react to him. He—of all men—could not affect her like this. She took a sip of the coffee before saying, "I don't think those kids were working for Luther."

She hoped they weren't, but then why had they been back in the emergency room area? Anita?

Had she looked the other way to allow them back? Had the security guard?

He hadn't wanted to let Clint through with his weapon despite his having a permit to carry, until he'd recognized him from when they'd been on the force together. Of course, even the chief thought Luther Mills had a mole in the police department. Maybe the security guard was friends with that mole.

Her head began to pound with all the possibilities. But she couldn't look for conspiracies everywhere. She couldn't live her life in constant fear.

"I can get you another prescription when I go to work today," she offered.

"You're not going anywhere."

"I told you that I can't stop living my life," she said. "I have rent and bills to pay. I have to work." More for her sanity than for the money. If she was locked up in a house all day with Clint Quarters, she would lose her mind for certain.

Or worse.

No. She was in no danger of losing her heart to Clint Quarters. Not to the man who had caused her brother's death.

"You have to testify," Clint said. "And if you don't stay here, you're not going to live to do that."

She sighed. "And here your boss convinced me you were the best bodyguard for the job."

"I am."

"You must not be that good if you don't think you can protect me if we leave here," she said, purposely goading him.

He narrowed his eyes. "I have protected you."

"So it's settled," she said. "I'll put on my scrubs." She'd found some loose yoga pants and an oversize T-shirt in the closet that she'd worn to sleep in. "And you'll take me to the hospital."

"No!"

She ignored him, set the mug back on the counter and headed toward the bedroom. But she didn't get far before a big hand wrapped around her arm and stopped her short.

"You're not going anywhere," he said.

She turned back and glared at him. "You're my bodyguard," she said. "Not my jailer. I'm not the one under arrest. Luther is."

"Rosie—"

Before he could say anything else, the panel next to the door buzzed. He tensed and removed his hand from her arm in order to draw his weapon.

Then a voice emanated from the speaker next to the door. "Hey, Clint, it's Landon. I've brought ADA Gerber to speak with Ms. Mendez."

"Good," Clint said as he holstered his weapon and walked over to open the door.

Maybe it was good for him, but it wasn't good for Rosie. She still intended to go to work. So with his hand removed from her arm, she headed into the bedroom and changed into her scrubs just as she'd intended.

Fortunately there was a washer and dryer in the master closet, so she'd washed them. They smelled fresh as she pulled them on. She clipped on her ID badge before opening the bedroom door again.

The three people in the living room must have been watching it because they were all staring at her as she stepped out. Clint had his coffee cup in his hand again as he leaned back against the counter.

Another man stood near him. He was even bigger and broader than Clint was, with thick, unruly-looking brown hair and brown eyes. That must have been Landon.

Ms. Gerber looked as gorgeous as ever in a suit with a tight skirt. Her black hair hung like a silk curtain around her slender shoulders. She looked more like a model than an assistant district attorney.

Even though Rosie had showered and washed her clothes, she still felt dowdy around her. "Why are you here?" she asked the young lawyer, although she could guess. Clint had called her.

The first thing the woman said was, "You need to stay here."

Rosie glared at Clint, who didn't even acknowledge her now. And she knew she'd guessed right.

But the woman wasn't prosecuting Rosie. She couldn't sentence her to remain behind bars or reinforced steel doors. And if she tried, she would be a damn hypocrite. Rosie wasn't afraid to call her one.

"What about you?" she asked the ADA. "Are you staying in a safe house?"

Jocelyn shook her head. "It's not necessary for me," she replied. "You're the only witness. If *you* die, the case is over. If I die, someone else will just take over the case. So it makes no sense for Mills to kill me."

"Unless the DA on his payroll takes over the case," Landon said.

And Jocelyn glared at him as if she hadn't appreciated his input. Were bodyguards supposed to be seen and not heard?

Wasn't that the way movie stars and other celebrities treated them?

But Rosie wasn't any kind of celebrity. She shouldn't need a bodyguard at all. Having a police officer follow her around had been bad enough. But at least he had just followed her; he hadn't tried telling her what to do and not do.

"We're not talking about me," Jocelyn Gerber said.

"We're talking about the key witness for the prosecution."

"We're talking about me," Rosie said. "I'm a person with a life."

"A life you're going to lose if you don't stay safe," Jocelyn said. She glanced around the apartment. "And you're safe here. Far safer than you were staying in your own place where Luther knew where to find you whenever he was ready to get rid of you."

Rosie snorted. "You need to get to know Luther better if you intend to prosecute him. He can find me anywhere. He has people in the police department and in your office. You don't think that he already knows where I am? Where you are?"

Jocelyn shivered.

As well as being beautiful, she was smart. But she wasn't street-smart. She was book-smart. She hadn't grown up where Rosie had, how Rosie had. Rosie didn't need to know much about her to know that; the lawyer looked every bit as pampered as the judge's daughter had.

"She's right." Clint came to her defense, surprisingly. "Luther probably has eyes on this place already."

Clint was street-smart, and not just from the years he'd been a vice cop. Javier had told her that Clint had grown up not far from where they had…and not much differently. But maybe that was just a story he'd told her brother to inspire that hero worship.

The one thing she knew for certain about his past was that he'd spent years pursuing Luther Mills. So he knew the drug lord very well.

Clint turned toward her now. "That's why you can't leave, Rosie."

"No, you can't," the prosecutor chimed in.

"So you should stay here, too, Ms. Gerber," Landon remarked.

She glared at him again. There seemed to be as much animosity between the two of them as there was between Rosie and Clint. Rosie wondered what their history was, because they obviously had one.

"You said that the guards outside haven't seen anyone watching the place. You said no one followed us," Jocelyn fired back at Landon. Then her face flushed as she must have realized she'd just contradicted what Clint had said. She turned toward Rosie now. "That doesn't mean that Officer Quarters—that Clint—isn't right. You said so yourself that Luther probably already knows where you are."

Rosie nodded. "So there's no more reason for me to stay here than there is for you."

"You have to testify," Jocelyn said, and only now did she sound frightened. She wasn't worried about losing her life. She was worried about losing her case.

"I will testify," Rosie assured her.

"Not if you're dead," Jocelyn told her. "If you leave this place where you are safe, you're risking your life but most of all you're risking justice for your brother. Do you want his killer to go free?"

Rosie's stomach churned even though she'd had only a sip of that coffee. She rushed toward the master suite and the bathroom off it—afraid that she was going to be sick. But she already was—sick of being afraid. And sick of being with Clint Quarters.

"Damn it!" Clint cursed Rosie's reaction to the ADA's persistence. Her golden skin had paled, and as she'd run off, she'd looked like she was going to be sick.

"I'm sorry," Jocelyn Gerber said, but she sounded unapologetic. "She needed to hear it, though."

"It's too much," Clint said.

He could see that Rosie was overwhelmed. Her life had been turned upside down the minute Luther had pulled the trigger and ended her brother's life.

"Parker told us that you wanted Jocelyn to come here and talk some sense into the witness," Landon said, surprisingly coming to the defense of the assistant district attorney that no one in the vice unit had respected, least of all Landon.

Clint and Landon had often discussed her, not just at work but at the house they rented together. They hadn't liked her because she'd lost too many of the cases they'd brought her.

Had that been an accident? Or had it been on purpose?

Maybe Jocelyn was the leak in the district attorney's office. And Landon had brought her right to Luther's next victim. But if Jocelyn was really working for him, why would Luther have put out a hit on her as well?

"I wanted ADA Gerber to talk some sense into her," Clint said, "not manipulate her and make her feel guilty." He was the only one who deserved to feel guilty—he and Luther Mills. And Luther Mills didn't have the conscience or the heart to feel anything for anyone but himself.

"It will be her fault if Luther Mills gets away with her brother's murder," Jocelyn insisted.

Landon snorted now, and clearly whatever allegiance he'd felt for the person he was protecting was gone. "You're already setting up someone else to blame if you lose this case, too."

Her pale skin flushed. "I don't do that," she said. "I just want my witness to make it to the stand." She turned toward Clint now. "And if she doesn't, then that's your fault."

Landon opened his mouth on a curse word, but Clint cut him off. "She's right. It's my job to protect Rosie Mendez."

"Make sure you do your job," Jocelyn told him as she headed toward the door. "Because with her testimony, I won't lose."

"This time," Landon muttered as he trailed her toward the door. He reached around her and pressed the security code into the panel.

Had she seen that, too?

Because Clint wasn't entirely certain they should trust this assistant district attorney. Maybe she'd only had Luther mention her name so that she wouldn't look as if she were getting spared. Maybe that was why she didn't seem the least bit afraid for her life.

Clint was afraid for Rosie's. Very afraid.

Parker hadn't slept well the night before, even after making love to his gorgeous and generous wife. He suspected that he wouldn't sleep well until Luther Mills's trial was over and the scumbag had been sentenced to spend the rest of his miserable life behind bars.

He was too worried right now about the hits Luther had put out and about his team. He had no doubt that

Luther would love to take out every one of Parker's team along with his original targets.

Parker wasn't worried just about failing the assignment that his stepfather had given him. He was worried about losing his friends.

When his cell rang, he jumped, startled. He was nearly as edgy as he'd been when he'd had a hit out on his life years ago. His hand shaking, he almost knocked the cell phone off his desk as he fumbled to press the accept button.

"This is Parker," he answered the call.

"Landon," the caller identified himself.

"Everything all right?"

The hesitation had the short hairs lifting on Parker's arms. "What?" he asked anxiously. "What is it?"

"I…think we're being followed," Landon said, and he sounded distracted as if his attention was elsewhere. Probably on the rearview mirror.

"You have backup," Parker reminded him. "I'll have them intervene."

"I can lose whoever this is tailing us," Landon assured him.

"Good." Landon Myers was one of the best cops Parker had ever worked with. He didn't doubt that he could. "So what's the problem?"

"I'm not sure where I picked up the tail," Landon said. "They're good."

"So what are you saying?" Parker wondered. "That whoever is following you probably isn't some of Luther's flunky drug dealers?"

Landon uttered a ragged sigh. "I hadn't thought of that, but it's true."

"They could be cops," a female voice murmured.

Jocelyn Gerber would probably prefer to think the only leak was in the police department and not hers. But that wasn't possible. Unfortunately Luther had compromised both the police and the prosecutor's office.

"I don't know who the hell they are," Landon said, his voice gruff with irritation.

He wasn't any happier to be protecting Jocelyn Gerber than Rosie Mendez was to have Clint protecting her. Maybe Parker should have switched the bodyguards. But in his gut, he knew he'd assigned them correctly. And his mother had convinced him to always listen to his gut.

Because he'd listened, he knew no one would protect Rosie like Clint would. The former vice cop felt like he owed her because her brother had been his informant when Luther murdered him.

Parker's head began to pound as he tried to figure out the real reason for Landon's call, if he wasn't worried about losing the tail. "If you don't need backup to intervene, why did you call?"

Landon rattled the phone with another ragged-sounding sigh. "I might not have noticed them earlier."

"Okay..."

"We just left the safe house," Landon said. "We just left Clint and the witness."

Of course. Parker had sent them there—at Clint's request. He cursed as he finally understood Landon's concern. He was worried that he might have put the witness and his friend in danger.

"You think you might have led them there?" Parker asked.

"I don't know if I led them there," Landon said, "or if they were already there."

Landon must have had his phone on speaker because Parker could hear Jocelyn Gerber talking. "Rosie and Quarters said that Luther Mills probably already knew where they were."

And knowing Luther Mills, the drug dealer probably did. He had people everywhere—not just in the police department or district attorney's office, but everywhere.

They'd protected enough clients at that particular safe house in the warehouse district that Luther could have heard where it was, if he'd heard that the Payne Protection Agency was protecting the people he'd threatened.

So if he knew where Rosie and Clint were, it was only a matter of time before he made a move on the safe house. Then they would all learn just how safe it was.

How much danger were Rosie and Clint in?

Chapter 8

Rosie pressed her trembling hands to her face as she leaned over the side of the bed and drew deep breaths into her aching lungs. She needed to calm down, or she was going to have a full-fledged panic attack. Already her breathing was shallow and too fast; she was nearly panting for air.

Maybe she needed a paper bag to breathe into.

Or a Xanax.

Or hot and sweaty sex with Clint Quarters.

"Are you okay?" a deep voice asked.

She jumped and would have fallen off the bed had strong hands on her shoulders not caught and steadied her. So much for locking the door. Clint Quarters had still managed to get inside the master suite with her.

"No, I'm not okay," she murmured. She was losing her damn mind. How could she want him so much?

She hated him.

Didn't she?

"I'm sorry," he said.

She turned then to where he sat behind her on the bed and studied his face. "For what?"

He sighed. "I guess there are so many things I'm sorry about when it comes to you."

Kissing her? Was he sorry about that? Because she was sorry that it had happened. But even more sorry that it had stopped.

"What are you sorry about this particular time?" she asked him.

"I didn't mean for the assistant DA to upset you like she did," he apologetically replied.

She knew that; she'd heard him through the door. "She wants to win." And Jocelyn Gerber thought she needed Rosie in order to do that. Was the rest of her case that weak?

"It shouldn't be about winning or losing," Clint said.

And Rosie laughed at his naïveté. Maybe he had lied to Javier when he'd told him that he'd grown up like they had.

"What?" he asked.

"Everything's about winning and losing, isn't it?" she asked.

"It should be about justice," he said. "Justice for Javier."

"You wanted to take down Luther way before he killed my brother," she reminded him. "You were obsessed with it."

"For justice," Clint said. "Luther has hurt a lot more people than your brother."

There was something in his voice, something that

made her want to look at him more closely, but to turn fully toward him she had to swing her legs onto the bed. Now they were sitting side by side, her hip nearly touching his, her thigh nearly touching his as they shared the same bed.

"Who?" Rosie asked. Clearly, Clint was referring to someone specific. Someone he'd known.

He shrugged. "I don't remember all their names. But Luther Mills definitely has a list of victims a mile long."

She reached out and clasped his hand. "No. Who did he hurt that you knew?"

Instead of looking at her, he glanced down at their clasped hands. He probably couldn't believe she would willingly touch him, and this time wasn't to check a wound. At least not a physical one.

But she suspected he had an emotional one. She'd heard it in his voice, in the gruffness of it. Was it a lover? Had he lost a girlfriend to Luther? To drugs?

"My cousin, Robbie," he said.

"You were close?" Rosie had had no family but for her mom and her brother. Her maternal family had disowned her mother once she'd become an addict. And Rosie had barely known her father, let alone any of his family.

Clint nodded in reply to her question. "I lived with him when I had to move in with my aunt and uncle."

"When and why did that happen?" she asked. She shouldn't have been interested in anything about Clint Quarters. Maybe she was only asking because they were stuck together. Or maybe she *was* interested, more than she wanted to be.

He sighed, then chuckled. "You'll probably think it's funny."

"What?"

"That my parents were drug dealers."

"What?" she asked. "You were raised by people like Luther Mills?" And he had become a cop?

He chuckled again. "They were nothing like Luther. Or they wouldn't have gotten caught so easily. They were hippies—growing their own weed and enough for their friends."

They hadn't been drug dealers like Luther Mills then.

"That doesn't sound that bad." Especially now that marijuana had been mostly legalized, at least for medicinal purposes.

"They had a *lot* of friends," he said.

A giggle slipped out. And she pressed her fingers to her mouth. "I'm sorry."

"I said you'd think it was funny."

"I just can't imagine you growing up with peace and love and…"

"Homegrown?" He sighed. "I was fourteen when they were arrested, so I went to live with my aunt and uncle."

Her humor fled as she remembered the pain she'd heard in his voice. "How old was your cousin?"

"Thirteen," he said. "Just a little younger."

"So you were close."

He nodded. "Until I went away to college and he stayed home and started buying from Luther. But then he started to need more than he could afford to buy, so he started working for him, selling at the high school and then the community college he attended, so he could support his own habit."

He paused for a long moment—so long that Rosie had to prod him. "Then what happened?"

He sighed again, but his breath rattled with it. "He died."

"Luther killed him?"

"His death was ruled an overdose," Clint said.

But it was clear that he thought something else had happened. "You have your doubts."

"I guess it doesn't matter what really happened," he said. "Just like you blame me for Javier's death—"

"This is different!"

"No," he said. "You're right to blame me. If Javier hadn't been informing on Luther for me, he would be alive. I blame me, too."

She heard it in his voice, the guilt and regret. It should have made her feel vindicated in her hatred of him. But instead she felt a twinge of guilt because her resentment of him had only added to the burden of guilt he'd already put on himself.

He continued, "And if my cousin hadn't been using and dealing for Luther, he would be alive. So I blame Luther."

"It's not the same," she said. She saw that now.

But it was clear that Clint did not. He shook his head. "Both things were too dangerous for young men like Javier, like my cousin…"

He turned toward her now, sliding his fingers under her chin to tip up her face to his. "I'm sorry," he said again, and his voice shook with regret and guilt.

Again, she should have been happy. But she wasn't.

He was making it too damn hard for her to hate him. And she really needed to hate him.

If she didn't hate him, she might…

She closed the distance between their faces and brushed her lips across his. She'd meant it just as a gesture of comfort—because he was hurting so much. But quickly, passion ignited between them.

And he was kissing her back.

His mouth moved hungrily over hers, nibbling at her lips, parting them.

Her breath sighed out on a low moan. He was such a damn good kisser. He took away her breath and all of her common sense.

She wanted him in a way that she had wanted no one else. She wanted him so much…

Her fingers moved over the soft stubble on his strong jaw and then into the soft, soft golden hair on his head. She clasped his nape, pulling him closer so she could deepen the kiss. She slid her tongue into his mouth, tasting mint and coffee and a flavor that was his alone: one that she worried she could easily become addicted to.

He groaned as her tongue slid across his. And their tongues tangled together.

She moved her hands from his hair to his shirt. She wanted to tug it up and over his head. She wanted to see his chest again, and not as he was getting stitched up. But the shirt only went up as far as the holster he was wearing, revealing only his rock-hard abdomen.

He pulled back. Maybe he'd thought she was going for his weapon. Given how hateful she'd been to him since Javier's death, she didn't blame him if that was what he thought. But then he undid the holster and dropped it and his weapon onto the bed next to them. And he pulled his shirt up and over his head.

Rosie gasped. Not just because his chest was so damn sexy and muscular but because blood had seeped through his bandage. He should have let the resident put in more stitches.

But before she could tell him that, his mouth covered hers again. And his body covered hers as he leaned forward and pressed her back into the pillows. Her hands were between their bodies, her palms against his chest. The soft hair tickled her skin while his heart pounded hard and fast beneath one of her palms.

He trailed his fingers down her neck over the pulse that was pounding wildly with desire for him. Then he moved his hand even lower to cup her breast in his palm. Even though she was still wearing her scrubs and her bra, she could feel the heat and strength of his hand. And her nipple tightened, desire coursing through her body from it to her core.

She trembled beneath him.

And he pulled back.

Maybe he thought he'd gone too far.

And he had.

They had.

But then she felt what he must have felt first, his phone vibrating in the pocket of his jeans. He snagged his shirt and pulled it over his head with a groan. She didn't know if it was because his shoulder hurt or if it was because they'd been interrupted.

He strapped on his holster, too, before he reached for the cell, but when he did his hand was shaking. His voice was so gruff it was nearly unrecognizable when he said, "Hey, Parker."

He must have decided to take his boss's call in private because he stepped out of the master suite and closed the door between them. And Rosie lay back on the bed, panting for breath and praying for sanity.

If not for that call, what would have happened?

Would she have had sex with Clint Quarters?

She wasn't certain if that call had been a good thing or a bad thing since it had interrupted what might have happened. But it couldn't happen.

She couldn't have sex with Clint. She had vowed long ago to be nothing like her mother. So she had never been with anyone unless she genuinely cared about him. And she could never really care about Clint Quarters, not after what had happened to her brother.

Even he blamed himself for Javier's death.

But now she understood why he'd been so determined to take down Luther Mills. It hadn't been just to further his career, like she'd thought. It had been for justice for his cousin, just like she wanted justice for Javier.

But could she stay here—in this safe house—alone with Clint until the trial? Probably not without eventually having sex with him.

The attraction between them was too strong. Eventually it and he would prove too much for Rosie to resist.

Clint had had to close the door—so that he wouldn't toss down the cell phone and climb back into bed with Rosie. Tension gripped his body, making it ache more

than the fall into the dumpster had. He wanted her with
an intensity he'd never felt before.

And for a moment, he'd thought she wanted him
that way, too. The way she'd kissed him…

She'd seemed as hungry as he was. As needy.

He groaned.

"We don't know for certain that Landon was tailed
to the safe house," Parker said, as if trying to reassure him. He must have thought that was why Clint
had groaned.

He wished it was why.

"He could have picked it up after, or…"

"Or he picked it up here," Clint said. Landon was
good, so Clint suspected that was probably more likely
what had happened.

"We don't know that the safe house was compromised," Parker insisted.

"It doesn't matter where Landon's tail came from,"
Clint said. "Luther probably already knows where this
safe house is."

Parker's sigh rattled the cell phone. "I'm sure someone's probably informed him that Payne Protection is
guarding the witness."

"And we've used this place to protect clients too
many times," Clint said. "He would have easily been
able to find out where it is."

"We've used it so many times because it's secure,"
Parker said. "You need to stay there."

Clint hadn't mentioned anything about leaving, but
Parker knew him well from all the danger they had
faced during their years of working vice together. He
would know that Clint always liked to stay at least one
step ahead of a suspect.

He had to get Rosie out of here, and not just because Luther might have his crew make a move on the safe house. He had to get her out of here because if they stayed alone together, he might make another move on her. When Parker had called, he'd felt like a kid caught necking on his girlfriend's parents' couch. He had been acting like a teenager with no common sense and with no self-control.

Rosie already didn't trust him. If he used her situation and vulnerability to make love with her, she would never be able to trust him.

And he wanted her to—that was why he'd told her about his cousin Robbie. He wanted her to understand why he'd been so determined to bring Luther to justice. But it didn't matter what his reasons were; he had still cost Javier his life, Rosie her brother.

"Clint," Parker called out from the cell phone. "Don't do anything stupid."

It was already too late for that advice. Clint had been stupid when he had kissed Rosie the first time, in the hospital parking lot, because now all he wanted to do was kiss her again. No, that wasn't all he wanted to do. He wanted to do so much more to Rosie Mendez.

But the only thing he could do was protect her.

"Don't worry," he told his boss. "I've got this."

But then the door opened to the master suite and Rosie stepped out, her hair still tousled from his pressing her into the pillows, her face still flushed, her eyes still bright.

And he knew he had nothing. No common sense. No self-control. Whatever she wanted, he would be helpless to refuse. He could only hope that she wanted him as much as he wanted her.

* * *

Luther studied the man sitting across the table from him. His hair was slicked back, his suit tailored. He was the epitome of the word *shark*. The kind of lawyer people like Luther—who could afford the best—hired.

But he wouldn't need him. He wasn't going to have to worry about preparing a defense.

"You need to help me out," the lawyer implored him. "The case against you is strong."

Luther shook his head. He wasn't worried about whatever Jocelyn Gerber had put together.

"There's an eyewitness to the murder," the lawyer continued.

As if Luther didn't know.

As if he hadn't been aware that he'd gunned down Rosie's brother right in front of her.

She'd needed to know that was what happened to people who crossed him. Like Javier and Clint Quarters.

But she'd gone to the police. She'd told them what she'd seen. She had learned nothing from the message he'd tried to give her. And now she'd crossed him. That was unfortunate. He'd always had a thing for sweet, sexy Rosie. Too bad he would never get the chance to act on that now. She would be dead soon.

"The witness will not be a problem," Luther assured his lawyer.

The guy groaned, and his face flushed. "I can't know anything about that."

"You don't," Luther assured him.

"But the witness isn't the only problem," the lawyer said. "There's DNA and other physical evidence."

Luther leaned back in the chair and crossed his arms over his chest. "Don't worry about that, either."

The Payne Protection Agency was not going to stop him from getting the case against him tossed out. First, he would get rid of the witness, and then all the others would follow…along with anyone else who had the bad sense to cross Luther Mills.

Chapter 9

What had happened to Clint?

Rosie hadn't expected him to actually agree to leave the safe house. But he hadn't just agreed; he'd suggested it. He must not have cleared it with his boss or with the other guards, though, because he'd sneaked her out a back way of the warehouse through what had appeared to be someone's art studio. He hadn't given her any time to admire the colorful canvases, though, before he'd led her out of the warehouse and to the SUV parked on the street.

"Get in," he said as he opened the passenger door for her. But he didn't touch her. And she was glad of that. She didn't know what she might do if he touched her again. And yet she wanted him to touch her again. And again...

"Hurry," he told her.

So she complied, sliding onto the seat before slamming the door closed. He was around the hood in a second and jumped into the driver's seat. As he jammed the key in the ignition and turned it, he winced. The shoulder was still bothering him, obviously, though he was probably too proud to admit it. He pulled the SUV away from the curb and careen-ed around the corner, then around another. As he drove like a maniac, he kept glancing into the rearview mirror.

To make sure nobody was following them?

"What's wrong?" she asked. "Do you think Luther got to someone in the Payne Protection Agency?"

"Not on Parker's team," Clint replied. "I worked vice with all those guys. Every one of them wants Luther behind bars as much as I do."

After learning about his cousin, she doubted that. But she didn't argue with him; she didn't want to bring up his loss and his pain again.

"So you don't trust some of the other bodyguards?" she asked.

He shrugged and flinched again. "It's not just the guards I don't trust," he said. "The assistant DA…"

"Jocelyn Gerber?" she asked in shock. "You think Luther could have gotten to her?"

"It would make sense," he said. "She's lost a lot of cases that we brought to her. She might be setting this one up to lose, too."

Rosie shivered. She wasn't a big fan of Jocelyn's. She thought the woman was so ambitious that she cared only about winning. So why had she lost so many cases? Because she'd been paid to lose?

"She was threatened, too," Rosie remembered. That was why she had a bodyguard of her own. Yet she hadn't seemed very worried about herself. At the time Rosie had thought she was just being brave. But now…

"Yeah, she was singled out with you and the others," Clint confirmed. "Who knows? Maybe she hasn't been compromised. But we don't know who has been."

They didn't. They knew only that Luther had not and could not get to either of them. Clint hated the man for the same reasons that Rosie did.

Ironically, although he was the last bodyguard she would have wanted, Clint Quarters was probably the only one she actually could trust.

So she didn't want to lose him.

But that was the only reason why…

She wanted justice for her brother. And because she wanted to testify against his killer, she had to make sure that Clint was really okay, so that he would be able to protect her.

"We need to go to the hospital," she said.

"You can't work," Clint said. "It's too dangerous— for you and for the patients."

"It's too dangerous for the patients if the hospital is short-staffed," she said. "And it's not like armed gunmen would get past security anyway." She doubted that, even if those kids had been working for Luther the night before, that they'd been armed. They'd probably just been looking for her to tell others where she was.

"The hospital security is short-staffed, too," Clint said. "They wouldn't be able to stop as many gunmen as showed up at your apartment the other night."

Probably not. But she doubted that even Luther's crew would risk trying to kill her at a busy hospital where there would be so many witnesses to her murder. Even Luther wouldn't be able to get rid of that many witnesses.

"I doubt that would happen," she said. "But I'm not just concerned about missing my shift. I'm concerned about you."

He glanced over the console at her, and his deep green eyes were narrowed with suspicion.

"Yeah, I don't believe I care, either," she told him. "But you're protecting me. And that's going to be hard to do if you develop an infection or drop dead from blood loss."

"What—"

She reached over the console now and touched his shoulder. And a curse slipped through his lips.

The shirt was damp with blood that had seeped through that bandage. Because the shirt was black it wasn't noticeable just from looking at him, but he was still bleeding.

"You need more stitches," she said. Then she moved her fingers to his forehead. His skin was warm. "And probably some antibiotics."

Not to mention painkillers, which he'd already refused. Maybe because of his cousin and his parents, he avoided taking drugs. Rosie did for the same reason—because she was worried she might become an addict like her mother. And she had vowed long ago to never be anything like her. She'd vowed to be dependent on nothing and no one.

He shook his head and insisted, "I'm fine."

"No, you're not."

Despite the cool autumn day, he hadn't turned on the heaters. The SUV was cold inside, but sweat beaded on his lip and forehead. He had to be burning up.

"The dumpster was gross," she reminded him. "You are probably developing an infection."

"Luther will definitely have people looking for you to show up at the hospital," he said.

"You don't know that those kids were working for him," she said. "They could have just been there with a friend."

Teenagers came into the ER all the time. Usually they got hurt doing some dumb stunt to become internet celebrities. Or they were part of one of the many gangs in River City.

"Maybe they weren't working for Luther," he agreed. "But anyone else could have been, even that nurse who was chatting you up at the desk."

"She was curious about you," Rosie said. And she couldn't blame Anita for that curiosity. Clint was the kind of man who made a woman curious—about his past, about his life, about his looks, about how he kissed...

Desire coursed through her as she relived those kisses.

Clint glanced across at her. The shoulder must have been bothering him more than he wanted to admit because he conceded, "We'll just stop at the ER. A doctor can look at my shoulder, and you can let personnel know that you won't be able to work until after the trial."

She wanted to argue with him, but she was afraid that if she did, he wouldn't drive to the hospital at all. So she just nodded as if she agreed with him even though she had no intention of taking a leave.

She couldn't afford it, and neither could the hospital, which was proved when the minute they showed up, she was implored to start her shift early. Two other nurses hadn't shown up for their first shifts. The waiting room was backed up; patients were hurt and scared that they might not be seen.

"I have to help out," she told Clint. She couldn't just walk away from people in need.

He shook his head. "This was a mistake. We need to leave. Right now."

A nurse at the desk glanced at them, her eyes going wide with surprise. Rosie was closer to Joanne than some of the others. She'd told the woman before that she didn't need a relationship because she didn't want any man trying to tell her what to do.

And here was Clint being all alpha-male bossy with her. She would have been furious with him if she wasn't aware that he was only worried about keeping her safe in such chaos. So she tamped down her anger and smiled at him instead.

"Sweetheart," she said. "You need to get more stitches and some antibiotics. While you're getting them, I can help out with some other patients." Then before he could argue any further, she waved over the young resident who'd seen him the night before—or earlier that morning, whenever it had been.

"He discovered he's only human," she told the doctor. "He's still bleeding, and I think he's gotten an infection. I can hang an IV of antibiotics and plasma."

The doctor nodded. "You do that," he agreed. Some of the residents refused to listen to nurses because they didn't respect them. Others relied on them too much.

This resident tended toward the latter. "I'll get over to check the stitches as soon as I can. We're busy as hell."

That was often what they called the ER: hell.

"This is a bad idea," Clint whispered as he kept glancing around the overcrowded area. But he followed as she led him to a gurney.

"Take off your shirt," she told him.

That was a bad idea, too. Seeing him without his shirt did something to her, like give her amnesia, because she forgot all about their past and focused only on the present and how damn sexy he was.

He was careful when he removed the jacket he wore over the shirt, taking the holster with it. He sat it next to him on the gurney, so the weapon was within reach. She didn't believe he would actually need it, though.

Not here.

Then he took off the shirt.

And she had to remind herself—not here. She couldn't climb all over him here. But then she forced her gaze from his muscular chest to his shoulder.

The bandage was completely saturated, blood streaking beneath it to trail down the heavy muscles in his arm. She removed the bandage slowly and carefully, so that she wouldn't tug loose any of the stitches, but they were already loose, the skin swollen and red. It wasn't just red. Along with the blood, the pus of infection oozed from the wound, just as she'd feared.

She rushed around, grabbing an IV stand and putting in an order for the fluids.

Clint glanced uneasily at his nasty-looking shoulder. "Is it bad?"

"It's not good," the resident said as he joined them. "Guess you aren't a superhero." He didn't sound all that disillusioned, though. "Good call," he told Rosie, "bringing him back. Who knows what that infection could become."

He turned to Clint then. "You'll need to stay here for a while for the IV antibiotics."

"I'm not checking in."

"Hell, no," the resident agreed. "We don't have the beds. But this gurney will be yours for a few hours. You're lucky you have connections, or you'd be bleeding out in the waiting room with the others."

A nurse called out to him from behind a curtain.

"I'll be right back to redo the stitches," he said as he rushed off.

Rosie had automatically donned gloves before reaching for Clint's arm. But as her fingers touched his skin, even through the latex, she was aware that this was him. His skin, his body…

Her fingers trembled slightly tapping at his vein before piercing it with a needle. Despite her uncharacteristic clumsiness, he didn't even flinch. "Sorry," she murmured.

"Figured you owe me," he said.

She knew now that he blamed himself as much for Javier's death as she did. Maybe more.

She hooked the IV into the needle. "If that were the case, I wouldn't be worried about you." Someone called out for her, but before she could move away, Clint caught her hand.

"We can't stay here," he said.

"You have to," she reminded him. "You need these antibiotics."

He had his hand on the IV line as if he were about to tug it out. "I don't like drugs."

"These aren't those kind of drugs," she assured him. "You'll be fine."

"I'm worried about you."

She gestured at the area around them. "I'll be right here," she said. "You'll be able to see me and see that I'm fine." She didn't wait for him to agree, just rushed off to the other nurse who'd called out to her.

"That man of yours is fine," the woman remarked with a whistle of appreciation as she gazed over at the bare-chested bodyguard.

That was all he was to Rosie. Just a bodyguard. Not her boyfriend. Rosie had to remind herself of that—repeatedly—as she caught glimpses of him as she moved around the ER, helping treat patients.

He was seething. She could feel his anger across the space separating them. And maybe that was why he was angry—because she didn't come close to him again.

She didn't dare. For one, he would want her to leave. For another, he was too damn good looking, and she couldn't be near him and not want him. So while he was being treated, she kept busy.

Her heart pounded fast and hard just from knowing Clint was in the same area and that he was watching her. She pulled back the curtain around the next gurney and found a teenager sitting alone in the space. His shirt was torn and streaked with blood. She looked around for the ER laptop to pull up his intake information.

Had he been in a car accident?

A fight?

"Are you alone?" she asked him. So many kids

came in without parents—because they didn't have parents who cared, like her and Javier.

And Clint.

"Are you alone?" he asked her.

She smiled. She was used to the defensiveness. That was how you survived the streets around here; you acted tough, tougher than you really were.

But then he continued, "Or is your damn bodyguard with you?"

She knew, even before he pulled the knife on her, that this was no patient. He was one of Luther's crew—sent to kill her.

Clint had been right. It was too dangerous for her to come to the hospital. But she was afraid she would never get the chance to tell him he'd been right.

He would know when he found her body. And then he would blame himself just like he did for Javier's death.

Rosie had lied to him. Clint couldn't see her. She kept disappearing behind those thick vinyl curtains, like she just had again. All Clint could see were her tennis shoes beneath it. So he noticed as she took a quick step back and then stumbled forward as if someone was jerking her around. Or fighting with her.

He hadn't been able to see who was behind that curtain with her. She'd barely pulled it back before slipping behind it. She was so damn concerned about everyone's privacy when she needed to be concerned about protecting herself.

No. Clint was supposed to do that. But he couldn't when he couldn't even see her. Or whatever the threat might be against her.

Anyone could be behind that curtain with her. Clint should have never let her out of his sight. Hell, he never should have agreed to come to the hospital in the first place—no matter how bad he'd started feeling.

He felt better now, though. Stronger.

He pulled the IV from his arm, pulled his shirt over his head and his freshly bandaged shoulder. Then he grabbed his coat, so that his hand was on the holster and his weapon.

He had a feeling he was going to need it.

"How the hell did you let him just slip out?" Parker demanded to know from the guards standing around the empty safe house.

He'd had a feeling—that damn Payne gut feeling—that Clint would ignore his orders. So Parker had shown up to check it out for himself. And he'd found the safe house empty and one of the SUVs gone.

Cole Bentler shook his head. "I didn't think he'd give us the slip. He's supposed to be protecting her, right? Why the hell would he take her out of the safe house?"

Parker cursed. "Because he thought she was in danger here."

Parker never should have called him about the tail Landon had picked up. But maybe Clint would have left anyway. He'd been after Luther Mills so long that he knew how the drug lord operated.

Those he couldn't buy, Luther either intimidated or killed. It would have been stupid to believe that Luther hadn't found out where Rosie was.

Once he knew where the witness was, Luther wouldn't hesitate to have her eliminated. Because of the size of the organization he ran, Luther would have enough manpower to take on even the Payne Protection Agency.

Maybe Clint had been smart to get Rosie out of here. But did he have a safer place to take her?

Would any place be safe from Luther Mills?

Chapter 10

The kid looked as scared as Rosie was. He was breathing hard, and his dark eyes were wild.

"You don't want to do this," she said, and hoped like hell that she was right.

But if he did want to kill her, he would have plunged that knife into her heart the minute she stepped behind the curtain with him. Instead he'd nearly let her slip away from him.

Before she could get away, though, he'd caught her. He grasped her wrist tightly now in one hand, which was clammy against her skin. If his other hand was sweaty, it didn't show in how steadily he gripped the knife in it. The blade was long and so shiny that it had to be sharp. And it was close to her now.

If she tried to break away from him again, she had no doubt that he would slash her with that blade.

Not just his hand was sweating. Sweat beaded on

his lip and streaked down his temples from his forehead. He was probably as scared as she was.

And she was pretty damn scared, her heart beating furiously in her chest.

"You don't have to do this," she told him.

He shook his head. "I don't have a choice, lady."

And she knew. He wasn't here because of money. He hadn't been paid to kill her. He had been coerced into doing this. Either his life had been threatened or the life of someone the kid cared about—like Javier had cared about her and she him.

Was that how Luther had gotten Javier to sell for him? They had never really talked about it. She had refused to believe he would work for Luther after she'd tried so hard to keep him away from drugs and most especially from the drug dealer. She had preferred to believe that Clint framed him—even though Javier had apologized to her.

Why would he have apologized if he'd been framed? She'd known the truth; she just hadn't wanted to face it.

That was becoming a dangerous habit for her. Because she'd known that Clint was right. She shouldn't have come here. And now she might lose her life because of her stubbornness.

She wasn't giving up on herself or on this kid. Maybe she could reach him.

"Who is it?" she asked. "Who is Luther threatening to hurt if you don't kill me?"

The boy's eyes grew wilder with fear, as if just her saying that would endanger whoever he cared about.

"I can get you help to protect whoever it is," she offered him.

Clint would help.

But would he be able to help her before this kid got up the courage to swing that knife? Or would he be too late?

The kid's brow furrowed. "What are you talking about? Wanting to help me? I gotta kill you, lady. That's the order." And now he lifted that blade toward her throat.

She needed to fight. To scream. To do something.

Or she would let down herself and most of all, she would let down Javier. He deserved justice, so she needed to testify against his killer. She needed to make certain that Luther went to prison the rest of his life for Javier's murder.

She was just opening her mouth to scream when the thick vinyl curtain ripped—torn loose from the metal track holding it up.

Both she and the kid gasped as Clint stepped into the space with them, his gun in his hand. "Let her go," he said through gritted teeth.

"Your bodyguard is here," the kid said as if she'd lied to him or betrayed him.

She'd never told him that Clint wasn't there. She just hadn't realized how closely he'd been watching her. But she should have known.

The kid had slipped closer to her now, and that sharp blade was pressed against her throat.

Rosie felt the sharpness as the blade pricked her skin. She held her breath, scared that any movement, even breathing, would cause that blade to sink deeper and cut the artery in her neck.

"Don't come any closer, hero," he warned Clint. "Or you'll just watch her die."

A muscle twitched in Clint's cheek, above his tightly clenched jaw. But he didn't move, not even to lower the gun he pointed at the kid.

"Lady, where's the back way outta here?" the kid asked.

"There isn't one," she lied. But then she felt the knife nick her skin, and she cried out.

"Don't lie to me!" he yelled, and in his anger, he gripped the knife a little more tightly against her throat.

The cut deepened so that she felt a trickle of blood. If it went any deeper that trickle would become a gush.

"You took your bodyguard out the back way last night," he said.

So this was one of the kids who'd been here the night before—one of the ones that Clint had suspected worked for Luther. He hadn't been wrong. She had.

About so many things…

"I'm sorry," she said. But it wasn't really the kid to whom she was apologizing.

"Take me there," the kid told her. "Get me the hell away from this guy."

He must not have liked the way Clint was staring at him so intently. Despite the sweat that nearly dripped from him now, he shivered.

And so did Rosie.

She knew what Clint wanted her to do, what she had to do.

"Sure, sure," she said. "I'll take you there, but I can't walk with that blade against my throat." She reached her arm up, closing her hand around the kid's wrist. He had already begun to lower the knife as she jerked it farther away from her throat.

Then she heard the gun blast, which was deafening and close. So close that she felt the rush of air as the bullet whizzed past her face and struck the kid's shoulder. The knife slipped free of his loosened grasp and clattered to the floor. Then the kid dropped to it as well.

Rosie screamed—in surprise at it all more than in fear. Instinct had her dropping to her knees next to the kid to assess his wound. How badly was he hurt?

Had Clint taken his life in order to save hers?

Clint picked up the knife. The sharp blade was smeared with blood. Rosie's blood. She was lucky to be alive. But she might not stay that way.

He reached for her arm, trying to pull her up from the floor. "We have to get out of here."

He doubted the kid was alone. He hadn't been the night before. There had been at least one other kid with him. Maybe even more of Luther's crew in the rest of the hospital or the parking lot.

"C'mon," Clint urged her. "You know Luther didn't send just this one kid after you. There is more of his crew here." Just waiting to finish what the kid had started.

She ignored Clint as she gestured for help. "He has a GSW," she called out to the rest of the staff, as if they hadn't heard the shot, as if they weren't standing around—their faces white—as they had watched it all play out.

They were frozen with fear—until finally the young resident moved, dropping to his knees beside Rosie. "Badass," he murmured again like he had the night before.

But Clint suspected the young man was talking about Rosie now, instead of him. She was badass.

If she hadn't gotten that knife away from her throat, she would have died. Clint wouldn't have been able to get the shot without the kid cutting her carotid artery.

The rest of the staff finally mobilized and rushed forward to help the kid. And the security guard, the same one from the night before—the retired cop—came up to Clint with his gun drawn. Where had he been when Clint needed backup?

Of course, he could have been there, and Clint might not have noticed. He'd been totally focused on that knife pressed so tightly to Rosie's throat.

The security guard held out his other hand for Clint's weapon. But Clint shook his head and grasped it tightly as he glanced around the busy ER.

"There must be others," he warned the guard. "You need to lock the place down, make sure nobody leaves." He could only hope that the other members of Luther's crew would leave instead of trying for Rosie themselves.

He wasn't sure the security staff would be much backup if Luther sent in a firing squad the size of the one he'd sent to her apartment. Clint had been right to not want to bring her to the hospital.

"Call the police," Clint said.

"You're the police," the guard said, no doubt believing that Clint was still with the River City PD.

But now he shook his head. "Not anymore. I'm private security for the Payne Protection Agency."

The guard reached for his gun again. "Then I need to take that."

Clint held tight to his weapon and to the knife. "I'm

on special assignment for the chief of police. Call Woodrow Lynch's office."

The guard's face flushed. "Yeah, right, like the chief would take my call."

"Tell him you're calling for me," he said. "Clint Quarters." He turned away from the guard to focus on Rosie. But she was gone.

Only a puddle of blood lay on the floor where the kid had fallen. That and something else…

He stepped closer to see what it was. He'd already picked up the knife. Now he picked up a cell phone. It wasn't Rosie's. She'd stowed hers in her purse and her purse in her locker when they had first arrived.

Where the hell was she?

While he'd been arguing with the guard, Rosie must have slipped away with the others who'd wheeled off the gurney with the kid on it. But where had she gone?

She wasn't a surgical nurse, if that was where they were taking the kid. And she wouldn't be responsible for taking him to the morgue, either. Not that Clint believed that gunshot wound would kill him.

Clint had only been trying to disarm him, so that he wouldn't hurt Rosie.

But while he'd been distracted, had someone else gotten a hold of her?

The guard better damn well hope no one had, because Clint would not be happy with him. But he knew who was really to blame if Rosie was harmed.

Luther Mills.

The man wouldn't have to worry about his trial if he hurt Rosie.

He wouldn't live to defend himself.

* * *

The ring alerted Luther to an incoming call on the drop cell. He hadn't bothered to silence the ringer. No one would dare to report him for having the phone. "Hello."

Hopefully this was good news. The news that Rosie Mendez was dead. But before he could ask, a deep voice said, "Hello, Luther."

"Ex-officer Clint Quarters," Luther said with a chuckle. "How did you get this number?"

More importantly, how the hell had he gotten the phone from which he'd called? That cell belonged to the kid who'd been ordered to carry out Rosie's murder. He had a sick feeling that hadn't happened.

A sick feeling that Clint Quarters had made certain that wouldn't happen. And now he knew Luther had a drop cell in jail. He had no doubt that Clint would report him. Officer Quarters had always been way too by the book, even more so than Parker Payne.

He'd been all about law and order.

Now he would have to destroy it, and yet he wasn't ready to end this call, not until he knew exactly what had happened to Rosie.

"I got it off the kid you sent to kill Rosie," Clint replied.

"I did what?" Luther asked, feigning innocence. "You must be mistaken."

"The mistake was all yours," Clint said. "We're going to nail you for witness intimidation."

"You're not a cop anymore," Luther reminded him. "You quit after you got your young protégé killed."

There was a long silence, so Luther knew he'd

scored a direct hit with remark. But he wanted to
know if his other hit had been successful. So he continued, "You're wrong, of course, about my wishing
sweet Rosie any harm. But has she come to any? Is
she dead?"

The silence continued so long that he realized Clint
didn't know. He chuckled. "What, have you already
failed in your new job as a bodyguard? Is she dead?"

"You better hope like hell she isn't," Clint said. "Or
you're next, Mills."

Luther chuckled again. He knew Clint's threat was
an idle one. His was not. Knowing that the call was
too short to have been traced or recorded, he said,
"No. You are."

Chapter 11

Rosie couldn't stop shaking. Her fingers trembled so badly that she was barely able to twirl the tumblers on the lock on her locker. She had come so close to getting killed.

So close to failing her brother.

The lock clicked open and so did the locker. She caught her reflection on the mirror inside the door. Her face was pale, her hair tangled around it, and on her neck was the wound where the blade had nicked her skin. The trail of blood from it had dried.

If it had cut just a little bit deeper, he might have hit an artery. Even in an emergency room full of hospital personnel, she could have bled out before anyone had had a chance to save her.

But Clint had.

He'd saved her.

He'd pulled back that curtain before the kid had worked up the courage to stab her. And she had no doubt he would have found the courage somewhere. Luther had been holding something over his head, something that had made him desperate enough to take a life.

To take her life.

She shuddered in horror at how close she had come to dying. But then strong hands gripped her shoulders, and the fear flashed through her again. She opened her mouth to scream, but it was too late.

A big hand clasped over it.

This was it. Clint had been right again. The kid hadn't been in the hospital alone. And whoever had been working with him had her now.

She couldn't expect Clint to save her this time. Somehow, she'd lost him when she'd helped take her attacker to an operating room. Clint had been talking to the security guard when she'd rushed off.

She should have let the others take the kid. She shouldn't have been worried about him. She should have been worried about herself.

But he was so young.

He'd reminded her of Javier.

Javier, like Clint, would have wanted her to protect herself, though. How could she do it now?

Could she reach the canister of Mace on the top shelf of her locker? She raised her arm and tried to snag it but the man holding her pulled her back, away from her locker. Then he turned her around to face him.

She didn't want to look at him. Maybe he wouldn't kill her if she couldn't identify him.

When the hand slid away from her mouth, she said, "Don't kill me. I promise I won't testify."

She was lying, though. And she was not a good liar. So she doubted her assailant would believe her. And even if he did, he wouldn't dare cross Luther Mills. He would kill her because he'd been ordered to—just like the kid in the ER had been.

"Where is she?" Clint asked the first person who stepped out of the OR.

"Who?" the man in scrubs asked. "We had a male on the operating table."

"Rosie Mendez. The nurse from the ER," he said.

"The one this kid attacked?" This man, with all the blood on his scrubs, must have been one of the surgeons. He shook his head. "She brought him down, then left."

On her own? Or had she been taken like the kid had tried taking her out of the ER?

He needed to find her. But first he needed to know if he'd taken a life. He'd had to before in his line of work, and it never got any easier. He gestured toward the operating room. "Did he make it?"

"Why do you care?" the doctor asked.

"Because I shot him."

The doctor gasped, then nodded. "Yeah, he'll be fine. But like I told the other detective, he won't be able to talk for a while yet."

Other detective? Was there really one at the hospital already? And had he been so impatient that he'd gone inside the OR during the surgery?

Who the hell was here?

Clint cared less about that, though, than he cared

about where Rosie was. Without another word he rushed back to the ER. He had no doubt that Rosie would resume her shift as if nothing had happened to her. She was that much of a professional caregiver.

But she was nowhere to be found.

The nurse who'd been working with her earlier caught sight of him, though. "She went into the locker room. HR told her to leave."

"They fired her?" Clint asked.

She'd nearly been killed. She shouldn't have been here to begin with; she shouldn't have been putting her coworkers and patients in danger.

The nurse shook her head. "Not Rosie. They just want her to take some time off, which she never has. They think she'll need it after this. That was a close call. Good thing you were here." The nurse narrowed her eyes with suspicion.

Good thing Rosie would not be working anymore. They hadn't fooled anyone about their true relationship. Maybe Clint had fooled himself. He had started to feel like her boyfriend. He cared about her as more than a witness.

He cared about her as if she were his girlfriend.

Not that he knew what it was like to have one of those. He'd always taken his job more seriously than any relationship, and thus every relationship had ended quickly.

No woman wanted to come second to a job. Once he'd become a bodyguard, he'd thought things might be different. That he might be able to make a life for himself.

But he hadn't felt right about that after Javier's life had ended. Had Rosie's?

Where the hell was she?

"Who are you really?" the nurse asked.

Because he had no intention of letting her work another shift before the trial, he answered honestly, "Her bodyguard."

The woman nodded, but then she narrowed her eyes again. "Are you sure that's all you are?"

No. He wasn't sure on his end. And even on Rosie's end, he was more than that. He was the man who'd gotten her brother killed. That was really all he would ever be to her. All he could ever be to her.

"I've known Rosie for a while," he admitted. "I knew her brother."

The woman nodded. And she hadn't shown any surprise that Rosie had a bodyguard. She might not have told anyone at the hospital, but they all knew about her brother, about Luther Mills and about the trial. "She's in the locker room," she said. "Do you know where that is?"

"Yes," he replied, and started toward it.

So he almost missed her next comment: "I had to show the other man where it was."

Alarm struck him like a blow to his heart, making it beat faster. He turned back and asked, "Other man?"

"The detective."

What detective? A real one or one of Luther's crew that was claiming to be one? Or worse yet, a real one who was one of Luther's crew?

He didn't ask her. She wouldn't know. He rushed off to find out for himself. As he pushed open the door to the locker room, he discovered that Rosie was not alone.

But it wasn't one of Luther's crew with her. It was

a real detective—Spencer Dubridge. And Clint seriously doubted that the serious detective could have any association with Luther Mills except for wanting him behind bars as much as Clint did. And even if he was working for Luther, he hadn't been able to hurt Rosie—because he was not alone.

Keeli Abbott was with him. She stood a distance from him, though, as if she couldn't stand being near him. And when she saw Clint, she shook her head. He couldn't tell if she was disgusted with him or with Dubridge, though.

"What the hell's wrong with you?" Spencer asked him. "You're supposed to be her bodyguard. Where the hell have you been?"

Heat rushed to Clint's face with embarrassment. He had no defense. He hadn't been doing his job very damn well.

Surprisingly enough, Rosie came to his defense. "He saved my life again," she said. "He shot the kid who was trying to stab me."

"I've already been to the OR to check on him," Dubridge said. "I didn't see you there. Where've you been, Quarters?" And he sounded suspicious of Clint, like he thought there was a reason he hadn't been doing the job, like he'd been hired to look the other way.

Damn Luther Mills and his leaks; he'd made everyone suspicious of everyone else.

Clint snorted. "I was locking down the hospital with the security staff. They're stopping everyone from leaving to search them for weapons. Something the police should be doing, but I didn't even realize they were here yet. How'd you get here so fast, Dubridge?"

And now he allowed the suspicion to enter his voice.

And Spencer laughed. "Touché."

"Yeah, whatever," Clint said. "Answer my question."

"Parker put out a call that you and the witness disappeared," Keeli said, and she sounded defensive of Dubridge, albeit begrudgingly.

Dubridge continued as if she hadn't spoken, though, as if she weren't there. He'd always treated her that way when they'd all worked vice together, too. "From the way she was talking the night before," he said, "about wanting to work, I figured she might be here."

That was why Spencer Dubridge had made detective at such a young age. The guy was smart and always a few steps ahead. That was why he'd been the one to catch Luther Mills, too. But he couldn't have done that without Rosie's help.

"The safe house might have been compromised," Clint said. "So we had to leave anyway."

Keeli nodded her blond head. "That's what Landon said." She grimaced. "He feels bad that he might have let someone tail him there."

"It wouldn't have mattered," Clint assured her. "Luther would have found the place."

"None of that explains what the hell you're doing here," Dubridge said.

"We stopped here to have his wound treated," Rosie added—again coming to his defense.

Spencer studied her scrubs. "And you weren't working?"

Her face flushed now. "Just helping out while he was being treated."

"Even if Luther knew where the safe house is, he couldn't have gotten anyone inside," Spencer said as if he knew the place. "No kid with a knife would have threatened her into no longer testifying."

Clint's heart jumped for a moment. "What?"

"She said she's no longer going to testify," Spencer said, and there was anger on his face and in his dark eyes.

Clint looked to Rosie, whose face flushed an even deeper shade of red. "I only said that because he grabbed me, and I thought he was working for Luther."

Clint's fingers curled into his palms as he fisted his hands. "You grabbed her?"

Maybe he was working for Luther.

But Keeli wasn't. Clint glanced at her, and she just shook her head again. He had no doubt this time whom she was disgusted with—whom she'd always been disgusted with when they'd worked together. Bodyguard Barbie, as Spencer had called her the other night, was flattering compared to the names she had had for him. Detective...

Had Parker purposely matched each of them up with the person they could stand the least? Of course, that was the reverse in his situation. It was Rosie who couldn't stand him.

"I thought she was running," Spencer said. "We need her, or Luther might get away with murder. She has to testify."

"I will," Rosie assured him. "I have no intention of not testifying."

Both men sighed in relief. Javier could not have died for nothing. His death would make sense only if it finally brought Luther Mills to justice.

Spencer was studying Clint now. Was he still suspicious of him the way Clint had been suspicious of him?

"Put away your interrogating-a-suspect face," Keeli told him. "Clint wants Luther Mills behind bars even worse than you do."

Rosie stared at the other woman, as if surprised that she knew how Clint felt about Luther. But everybody who worked with Clint knew how he felt about Luther. They just hadn't known why. Rosie was the only one who knew that now that Javier was dead. Her brother was the only other person Clint had told. Maybe that was why Javier had decided to become his informant. Maybe he really had manipulated him, just as Rosie had accused him of doing, just not in the way that she had thought.

"If that was true, why didn't you take the arrest for yourself?" Spencer asked. Then he glanced at Rosie, and he must have remembered. She'd said she would talk, but only to anyone other than Clint Quarters. He shook his head now and murmured, "What the hell was Parker Payne thinking?"

Clint had been wondering the same damn thing.

Then Dubridge focused on him again, as if they worked together, as if Clint were still his underling. "You have to make sure she lives to testify," he ordered him. "Get her back to that safe house. Parker has it secured like a fortress."

"If that was true, how the hell did we get out so easily?" Clint asked.

"Nobody was looking for someone trying to get out," Keeli said, in defense of their fellow bodyguards. "They were looking for someone to try to get in. And nobody has. It's safe."

A door opened and closed from somewhere inside the locker room. Since they didn't see anyone, that person must have been in the bathroom. They were not alone.

"Safer than here," Spencer added. Like Clint and Keeli, he had drawn his weapon.

After Rosie's nearly getting stabbed in the ER, Clint couldn't argue that she was safe here. But he wasn't sure where she would be safe.

Dare he trust that even if Luther knew where the safe house was that his fellow bodyguards would help him defend Rosie from an attack? He'd have to…because he'd nearly lost her here. He couldn't risk that happening again.

Parker hit the button on his steering wheel, accepting the call on his Bluetooth.

Spencer Dubridge's deep voice emanated from his speakers. "I found the witness," he said.

"We did," a female voice corrected him.

Spencer didn't have the phone on speaker, but Parker was still able to hear her. They must have been in a vehicle together.

"I didn't ask you to look," Parker reminded the two of them. "Dubridge, you're supposed to be under protection, too."

"I'm not in any danger," Spencer insisted.

"You nearly got Maced," Keeli corrected him. And she laughed as if she would have enjoyed seeing that.

"Yeah, some bodyguard you are," Spencer shot back at her. Then he spoke to Parker again, asking, "If you think I'm in so damn much danger, how come I got Bodyguard Barbie?"

"Stop calling me that!" she yelled at him, her voice echoing through Parker's speakers.

If Spencer didn't stop antagonizing her, he might be in more danger from his bodyguard than from Luther Mills. Parker nearly chuckled at the thought. But he held in his humor to hotly defend one of his top bodyguards. "Keeli Abbott is one of the best damn cops I've ever worked with, you included."

"Thanks a lot," Spencer snarkily replied.

"You could be working for me now," Parker reminded him. "I offered you a job."

"I have a job. And nobody's going to stop me from doing it," Spencer said. "Not you. Not Bodyguard Barbie and sure as hell not Luther Mills."

Maybe it was good that Spencer had turned down Parker's job offer. The man was too damn stubborn for his own good. So Parker focused on what he'd said at the start of their conversation. "You found the witness? Is she okay?"

"Yeah, just nearly got stabbed to death at the hospital by a 'patient.'" Clearly, the person had been no patient.

Fear stabbed his heart. "What about Clint?"

"He shot the kid."

"Good. Is he okay?"

"Yeah, the kid is fine," Spencer replied. "I talked to him the minute he regained consciousness after the surgeon removed Clint's slug from his shoulder."

"Clint," Parker specified. He had no sympathy for a killer. "Is he okay?"

"Yeah, just pissed." Spencer chuckled. "I sent him back to the safe house."

He was probably pissed that Spencer had been giving him orders. And Parker didn't blame him. Her voice was softer now, but he heard Keeli murmur something along those same lines.

"He's pissed that he nearly lost her," Spencer said. "I think he'll keep a better eye on her now."

Knowing how Clint felt about Rosie Mendez—even though he'd never admitted it—Parker doubted his gaze had ever left her. That was how she'd survived another attempt on her life—because of Clint.

"What about the kid?" Parker asked. "Did you get him to admit that Luther Mills hired him?"

Spencer snorted. "Hired him? Terrorized him is probably more like it. He says Luther had nothing to do with it. He was just grabbing the nurse to get him drugs. He claimed he's an addict."

"You don't believe him?"

"Cleanest addict I ever saw," Spencer said. And he'd spent quite a few years in vice, with them, before becoming a homicide detective. "He was after the witness, not drugs. And Luther must have ordered it."

"But we can't prove it," Parker surmised. "Just like every other damn time I've tried to take down Luther Mills."

"We can prove he killed the Mendez kid," Spencer said. "We just have to make sure the witness stays alive. Do you really believe Clint Quarters is up to the job of protecting her?"

Parker tensed. "I thought you said that he was okay. That he didn't get hurt."

"Not today," Spencer said. "But he's hurt from that fall out the window the night before. That's why they were at the hospital. His shoulder's pretty messed up."

"It didn't stop him from shooting her attacker!" Keeli yelled out from the background. That was part of what had made her such a damn good cop; she was a team player. Loyal and supportive.

Spencer Dubridge could stand to learn a thing or two from her.

And maybe he was, because he begrudgingly agreed, "No, Quarters did good today. But there will be another attempt. Luther isn't giving up until the witness is dead or until he's in solitary confinement."

Parker sighed. Spencer was right. If Clint was already hurt, this job might be too much for him. It might get him and the witness both killed.

Chapter 12

The silence in the SUV unnerved Rosie. She wanted to fill it with chatter, but she was afraid that if she opened her mouth she might cry. She was that exhausted and on edge.

She'd already been tired from not sleeping the night before. Then after what had happened in the ER and even in the locker room. For several tense moments, she'd thought that Detective Dubridge was one of Luther's crew determined to finish what his friend had started.

Then the blonde girl had intervened, telling him to let Rosie go or she would Mace him herself. Finally, he'd released her, but not before scaring her into lying to him.

The only way she would not testify against Luther Mills was if she was dead. Unfortunately, that was a distinct possibility, especially given the way that Clint kept looking in the rearview mirror.

"We're being followed," she surmised, and her voice only cracked slightly with the fear she was feeling.

"Yes."

"Thanks," she said.

His brow furrowed. "For what?"

"For being honest with me," she said. She would have hated if he had lied to her and tried to claim that everything was all right.

"If I'd told you nobody was back there, it would have been kind of hard to explain when I started driving like this then," he said as he jerked the wheel sharply and turned the SUV. He was going the wrong way down a one-way street. To avoid oncoming traffic, he jumped it over the curb and onto the sidewalk.

A scream of fear squeaked out of Rosie now. There were no pedestrians on this stretch of road, thankfully. The only thing Clint hit was a mailbox.

The corner of the bumper scraped against it as he took another sharp curve, veering back into traffic but going the right way. Then he turned again, to the left, and again, to the right. He zigzagged up and down the streets surrounding the hospital.

"I wouldn't have suspected anything," she said, and her voice went up and down with the movement of the SUV. "I thought you always drove like this."

Clint chuckled.

Rosie had one hand on the console and her other on the armrest as she bounced back and forth in her seat. Her stomach pitched like she was riding a roller coaster. She had never done well at amusement parks or even carnivals. Javier had always teased her about her weak stomach. She could handle blood and gore but not a kiddie ride at a street carnival.

This was no kiddie ride, though. And despite her attempts at humor, another little scream squeaked out between her trembling lips.

Clint's hand closed over hers on the console. "It's okay," he assured her. "We lost them."

Not we. He. She wouldn't have been able to drive like that. Hell, she rarely drove at all. She and Javier had never owned a car. And her mother certainly hadn't.

Rosie always took the bus.

"Who were they?" she asked. He hadn't just lost his backup again, had he? She wasn't sure if that was a good thing or a bad thing, though.

She wasn't sure who to trust anymore. Except for Clint.

"I don't know," he said with a shrug. "But I wasn't taking any chances."

"Then why are we going back to the safe house?" she wondered.

He sighed. "Spencer said Parker ordered it."

She'd been there. She'd heard him, but she hadn't been convinced. "And you believe him?"

Clint sighed again. "Yes. Parker didn't want me to leave it. And we shouldn't have."

"Thanks again," she said.

He glanced over at her, and his brow was furrowed in confusion again. "For what? Losing the tail?"

"For not saying you told me so about going to the hospital," she said. "You were right. It wasn't safe. Not for us and not for that kid or any other patients or staff." She'd put them all in danger. Tears rushed to her eyes, but she squeezed the lids closed to hold them in. She was not going to cry. She hadn't since Javier's funeral.

She wasn't going to now, because nothing was as bad as that, as burying her baby brother.

Clint's hand squeezed hers. "The kid is going to be okay. The bullet didn't hit anything vital."

"He'll survive being shot," Rosie agreed. "But will he survive not carrying out Luther's orders?"

"Would you have rather had him succeed on his mission for Luther?" Clint asked. "Because I know I'm damn glad that he didn't or you'd be dead."

"Why do you care?" she asked. "There's no love lost between us. Are you just like everyone else—determined that the *witness* live to testify?" She'd always known that he'd been determined to get Luther. Back then, she'd thought that it was just to further his career. Now she knew the real reason. Maybe she wasn't the only one.

That cute blonde bodyguard had seemed to know. And she'd certainly jumped to Clint's defense even against the man she was supposed to be protecting.

Something twisted in Rosie's stomach, making her feel sicker than she had when he'd been driving so erratically. But she couldn't be jealous of Clint Quarters.

Clint's fingers stroked over her hand now in a caress that had nothing to do with reassurance. "You're more than a witness to *me*, Rosie."

"Clint…"

"I know you hate my guts," he said, as if reassuring her. "But I don't feel that way about you at all."

How did he feel about her?

Before she could ask, he steered the SUV onto the

street in the warehouse district where the safe house was. She could ask him once they were inside the apartment, but maybe she should ask him before she went in with him.

Alone.

"I know you don't hate me," she said. Or he wouldn't have been risking his life for hers. "But how do you..."

"You're more than the witness," he said. "You're Javier's sister."

That was all she was—an extension of the guilt he felt over her brother's death. She should have been happy that he felt so guilty. But it didn't make her happy.

Since Javier had died, she hadn't felt any happiness at all. Maybe once Luther Mills was convicted of her brother's murder she would feel better. Justice for Javier would make her happy.

Not Clint Quarters. He could not make her happy. He would only ever remind her of what she'd lost.

"No," she said with a sigh. "They're all right. ADA Gerber, Detective Dubridge, your friends... I am just the witness."

But in this case, in the case against Luther Mills, the witness was the most important person. She didn't feel important, though.

She felt scared, and not just for her life.

Clint took his hand from Rosie's cold one. She was chilled and upset, and he couldn't make her feel better. Hell, just his presence usually made her feel worse.

He should have had Parker assign her another bodyguard. One she didn't hate. But he'd thought he would be the best one for the job because of his promise to Javier.

He'd nearly failed that promise. The mark on her neck, that trail of dried blood, had his stomach lurching with fear and regret. She could have died in the ER where she'd brought him for medical attention. And then he would have broken another promise to her brother.

No wonder she looked so scared. She wasn't the only one feeling fear. Clint was scared, too—scared that he was going to fail her and Javier.

And scared that he'd made another horrible mistake.

He'd lost the tail he'd picked up at the hospital. He had no doubt about that. But Luther's crew wouldn't need to follow him to the safe house if they already knew where it was.

They could be here, waiting for him.

Waiting for them…

Of course, the place was heavily guarded. That was why Parker and Spencer were so sure that it was the safest place for Rosie to be. Clint wasn't as convinced.

He hesitated to get out of the SUV and walk around to Rosie's side, so long that she murmured, "You don't want to be here, either."

He didn't. But he wasn't sure it was because he didn't think it was safe or if it was because he was worried about being alone with her again. If not for Parker's call earlier, he wasn't sure that he would have come to his senses.

He wanted her so badly. And in that moment, she had seemed to want him, too. Or had she only wanted to forget how much danger she was in?

Clint couldn't take advantage of that fear and vulnerability. He had to do the job he'd sworn he was able to handle; he had to protect her. So he needed to get her inside the safe house, and once they were inside he needed to keep his damn hands and his lips to himself.

He couldn't touch her again.

He couldn't kiss her.

Or he would only get distracted, so distracted that he might get them both killed. He was getting distracted now, so he forced himself to step out of the SUV. He needed some fresh air. Inside the SUV was full of her scent, vanilla and that spice she always smelled like.

But as his feet touched the sidewalk, the short hairs rose on his nape, and a chill chased down his back, between his shoulder blades. That chill wasn't just from the crisp autumn wind that had whipped up; this was a deeper chill—one of foreboding.

No matter what Parker and Spencer believed, it wasn't safe here, not for Rosie and not even for Clint.

He reached for his weapon just as shots began to ring out. "Get down!" he shouted at her.

But he didn't have time to jump back into the SUV. Bullets pinged off the metal of the vehicle and off the concrete near him.

And then one struck him, sending a searing pain down his arm.

And Rosie's scream rent the air.

He shouldn't have brought her back here. He'd only put her in more danger. And he wasn't going to be able to protect her if he was dead.

While Luther didn't have a TV in his cell, he had unlimited access to the television room. It helped that quite a few of the guards had drug habits, which they fueled by dealing to the prisoners and doing favors for their boss. While the county employed them as correction officers, Luther was their boss.

So he was hanging out alone in the TV room. Maybe there was a guard at the door, maybe not. He probably could have walked right out of the damn jail if he wanted.

He wanted…

It was taking his crew too damn long to get rid of Rosie and Clint. Maybe he needed to handle this little problem himself.

But if he just walked out of jail, he would become a fugitive.

He'd look guilty.

And while he was guilty as hell, he wasn't going to look it once Rosie was dead and that damn evidence had been destroyed. It was just a matter of time.

A breaking news report interrupted the program he'd been watching. A shooting in the warehouse district.

He leaned back and grinned.

This was it.

His crew had hit the safe house just like he'd ordered. With as many gunmen as he'd sent to the place, there was no way they could have failed.

Which the reporter confirmed when she said, "There are casualties…"

"There damn well better be," Luther murmured. He needed to end this now, so he could legally leave jail.

The scene behind the reporter showed a couple of zipped-up body bags. So at least two were dead.

Hopefully, those two were Rosie Mendez and Clint

Quarters. He took out a phone and stared down at it, willing it to ring with the confirmation of those deaths.

This was a different phone than the one Clint had called. He'd ditched that one in case the ex-cop had tried to trace it. Since this one was new, not all of his crew had the number yet. So he might have to wait a while to learn for certain that Rosie and Clint had died.

It had to be them. They could not have survived a third attempt, and not an attempt like this. He had sent an army after them.

Even Clint Quarters could not conquer an army.

Chapter 13

Rosie had thought the scene at her apartment, with all those gunmen, must have been what war was like. But she'd had no idea what war was like until the street outside the safe house had erupted with gunfire.

So many shots had rung out. So many bullets had been fired.

How many had struck Clint?

He was bleeding, but it hadn't stopped him from firing back, from jumping into the SUV and steering it away from the scene.

He'd run over at least one gunman. She'd heard the body strike the front bumper. Just as Clint had instructed, she'd been down on the floorboards. If she hadn't stayed down, she might have been hit because bullets had penetrated the windshield, had shattered the glass so that jagged fragments of it had rained down on Clint and even onto where she sat on the floor.

"We need to stop," she told him. And it wasn't just because the night air was whipping through the SUV, chilling her to the bone. He had to be even colder than she was. And he had to be hurt.

She wanted to know how badly. She wanted to help him like he had just helped her, saving her life once again.

But he continued to drive fast and erratically. With all the shooting, she couldn't imagine anyone had survived to follow them. Luther's crew must have been firing at them while Payne Protection bodyguards had fired back at Luther's crew. It couldn't have been Clint's fellow bodyguards firing at them.

Could it?

Had the safe house been a setup?

She hoped not, for Clint's sake. He had trusted and admired his boss. But Rosie knew all too well that no one was beyond Luther's reach. She'd had to face the fact that not even her brother had been.

"You've been hit," she said. Blood streaked down the side of his face from a wound on his cheek. It wasn't enough blood or a deep enough wound for a bullet to have entered. He must have just been grazed.

But his shoulder was bleeding again. From the old wound or a new one?

Was he in shock?

Why hadn't he spoken since he'd yelled at her to get down? What was wrong with him?

Maybe he had other injuries that she couldn't see from where she sat on the floor, with him across the console in the driver's seat.

"We need to go to the hospital," she persisted.

"Because that went so well for us last time," he replied, his voice heavy with sarcasm.

Despite the snark, she breathed a sigh of relief that he had finally spoken.

"Are you okay?" she asked again, and she tried to move up from the floor.

But he held out his hand as if to push her back down. "I don't know if we're safe yet," he warned her. "Stay where you are."

"I'd be safer belted into my seat if you crash this vehicle," she pointed out. "You shouldn't be driving."

"I'm not hurt that badly," he said.

But he was hurt.

Concern filled her just as it had when those shots rang out the minute he stepped out of the SUV. They'd been waiting for him—whoever had fired those shots. Had they just wanted him out of the way so they could get to her? Or was there a hit out on him as well?

She wouldn't put it past Luther to have put one on him. Hell, he'd probably already had one on him. He'd hated Clint even more than she had. She had no doubt that he probably wanted the former vice cop dead.

Fear overwhelmed her, but she fought it back with humor so that she didn't become hysterical. "You shouldn't be driving because you drive like a lunatic," she told him. She climbed up from the floor now, and he didn't push her back down.

She stared out the windows at the unfamiliar area. "Where are we?"

He hadn't been driving that long, but he'd been driving fast so he must have gotten them farther than she thought. They were definitely not in the city anymore, not with the thick woods on either side of the road.

Rosie was a city girl through and through. She'd been born in the city and had grown up there. She was used to sidewalks, not deep ditches and trees so thick that she couldn't see behind them. But she suspected there were no houses behind all of those trees, because there were no driveways.

She suspected there were only more trees.

Her heart had already been racing from all the gunfire. Now it began to pound even faster. She wasn't comfortable with isolation, especially when she was about to be isolated with Clint Quarters.

Then he turned the steering wheel.

And she grabbed for the armrest and console, certain he was about to drop them into one of those deep ditches. But a culvert of some sort was in this ditch, with a scattering of gravel and dirt on top of it. The SUV bounced down a path that wound between all those trees. It wasn't a driveway. Driveways to her were either made of concrete or asphalt. This didn't even have much gravel on it, just a smattering of stones on top of mud and deep ruts.

The SUV bounced again with such force that Rosie's head struck the roof of it. And Clint grunted in pain from all the jostling.

"We don't have to go to the hospital where I work," she said. "But we need to go to one."

And she doubted there was one in the middle of the woods. "You need medical treatment."

"I have a first aid kit," he said.

She glanced around the SUV. "Where?" She needed to stop his face from bleeding. His golden beard had turned red with his blood.

"There," he said. And he pointed toward a log cabin that suddenly appeared in the middle of the woods.

"Where are we?" she asked.

"Home."

This was not what she would have expected from Clint. Sure, he'd admitted his parents had been hippies. So maybe there was some of that nature lover in him as well. But still...

This didn't look like a place a man like him would choose to live. Alone.

But then again, maybe it was exactly a place a man like him would choose to live. Alone. Because despite his friendships with the other former vice cops–turned–bodyguards, he was a loner.

Clint had taken her home. Not that he could really call it that. He'd bought the place when he'd quit the force, but he hadn't moved in much of his stuff yet. And he hadn't spent many nights there, either. He mostly stayed in the city with Landon at the house they'd rented together when they'd both still been in the vice unit with River City PD.

He had been at the cabin recently to stock the kitchen and bring in some other supplies. He'd thought it could prove a good place to bring a potential client if the other safe houses were ever compromised.

He'd never imagined that Rosie Mendez might be the client he'd bring here one day. He'd never imagined Rosie in his home. She had yet to get out of the SUV even though he'd come around it to open her door.

He'd parked it inside a lean-to beside the cabin. Piles of wood for the fireplace surrounded the lean-to, concealing the SUV from anyone who might have been looking for them.

"You're safe here," he assured her.

She narrowed her big brown eyes and stared at him, clearly skeptical of his claim. "Maybe from gunmen," she acknowledged, "but what about lions and tigers and bears?"

"There are no lions and tigers," he assured her.

"What about bears?" She glanced fearfully at the woods around the small cabin.

"I've never seen any here." Of course, he hadn't been home very many times, but he didn't share that with her.

She reached out, but not for him to help her down from the SUV. She skimmed her fingers along his cheek instead.

He flinched at the sting of the wound, but it was nothing compared to the first one he'd gotten. It probably wasn't even a bullet that had grazed his face; more likely it was a piece of glass from the shattered windshield. The SUVs had reinforced glass and metal, but those shooters must have been using special ammunition. The SUV had dents and dings and quite a few holes from the bullets that had hit it.

He studied her face to make sure she had not been hit. She was so beautiful, her skin such a warm, honey color and flawless. But her curly brown hair was tousled. "Are you okay?" he asked.

She nodded. "I'm fine, but you're not. There's a first aid kit inside?"

"Yes."

She jumped down then and slipped on the damp ground. Her body slid into his. Before she could hit the dirt, he caught her with an arm around her waist, bringing her body even closer to his.

His body tensed and hardened at the closeness of her soft curves. She must have felt his reaction, because she tensed as well.

"This is a bad idea," she murmured.

It was.

He shouldn't have brought her here. He shouldn't have chosen to be alone with her. But he wasn't sure who the hell he could trust right now, if anyone. Parker and Spencer had assured him the safe house would be safe.

But they'd been wrong.

By accident or design?

He wouldn't have believed Luther Mills could get to either of them. But Luther didn't just pay people off; he threatened them, too. And Parker with his beautiful wife and kids and his big family had a lot to lose.

Clint had nothing.

But this cabin.

And his life.

And as he stared down at Rosie, he realized he had something else to lose, if he hadn't already: his heart.

Parker ripped aside the crime scene tape surrounding the safe house and stormed up to the officers interrogating his bodyguards. He had questions of his own for them. "What the hell happened?"

He'd convinced Clint to bring the witness back here. He'd assured him that it would be safe. No wonder Clint hadn't been answering his calls. And Parker had started calling him the minute he'd heard the news—not on television but through one of the two-way radios the other guards at the scene had been wearing.

"We came under attack," one of the guards replied. But this wasn't just any guard. It was the man who would soon be Parker's brother-in-law.

Lars Ecklund was a giant of a man with pale blond hair and blue eyes. He was also a former Marine, which was why he worked for Parker's brother Cooper, who was also a former Marine and with whom Lars had served.

"Do you think they followed Clint here?" Parker asked.

Lars shook his head. "No. They must have already been here, hiding somewhere, waiting to ambush him."

"And you missed them?" he asked disparagingly.

A person stepped around Lars. Parker hadn't seen her because the big body of the former Marine had blocked her. Nikki Payne was petite like their mother, with auburn curls and big brown eyes and an indomitable spirit. "They had to be hiding outside the perimeter. We had the block around the warehouse covered," she said. "We can't contain the whole damn city. They came at us fast."

Parker shuddered at the danger his sister had been in. He would never get used to her being a bodyguard now. For years he and his twin Logan had kept her chained to a desk in Logan's office, which was the original one of the Payne Protection Agency. That was why she'd joined Cooper's when he'd started his own.

Logan never would have let her out from behind the desk, and neither would Parker if he'd had the choice. "Are you okay?" he anxiously asked her.

"Of course," she said, dismissing his concern.

"She took out at least one of them," Lars said with pride in his fiancée.

But Nikki didn't look proud. She looked regretful. "Not much older than a kid."

"But he knew how to use a gun." Lars touched his shoulder, which had at least been grazed, because his shirt was stained with blood.

Shame slammed through Parker that he hadn't noticed immediately that he had been hurt. But his shirt was a dark blue, so it had been harder to see the blood. "Oh, no, you were hit," Parker said. "You need an EMT!"

"I'm fine," Lars said.

"Was anyone else hurt?" Parker asked anxiously.

The initial report he'd received had made it sound as if none of his team—and his brothers' teams—had even required medical attention.

But there was a long hesitation in which neither Lars nor Nikki would meet his gaze.

"What?" he asked. "Who else got hurt?"

"Clint," Nikki replied. "The minute he got out of the SUV they started firing at him like crazy."

"How badly?" Parker asked, his heart beating slow and heavily with dread.

Lars shrugged, then flinched. "Not bad enough that he wasn't able to return fire and take out at least one of the shooters before getting back into the SUV and speeding off."

Just because he'd left didn't mean that he was fine. He could have been fatally injured. Maybe that was why he hadn't been accepting Parker's calls. It wasn't because he was mad. It was because he was dead.

"And what about the witness?" he asked.

Nikki and Lars both shook their heads. "I don't know. The SUV came under heavy fire. And these shooters had special ammo—like someone knew about the reinforced metal and glass on our SUVs."

How the hell had someone found out about the safe house and the SUVs? Was someone within the Payne Protection Agency working for Luther Mills?

"It could have been hit," Nikki continued, then heavily added, "She could have been hit, too."

So they both might be dead.

He cursed.

And another curse echoed his. He turned around to find that his stepfather had joined them. And Woodrow Lynch didn't look pleased.

Parker wasn't worried anymore about having failed this assignment. He was worried about having failed a friend. He'd assured Clint that he would be safe if he brought the witness back here.

And Parker couldn't have been more wrong.

Chapter 14

Rosie walked across the front porch and through the door Clint held open for her. The cabin was small, probably just the one room, since a bed stood in a corner of the open space. The four-poster bed was on one side of the big brick fireplace while a couch stood on the other side of it. The kitchen and a small table took up the other half of the area. A door off the back of the open space opened onto a bathroom, but it looked like an add-on. So the place probably hadn't even had indoor plumbing until that addition.

Rosie turned back to Clint, who still stood near the door. "Is this really your home?" she asked. For a while, she'd thought he was a liar, had even told his boss that he was. But she had begun to doubt that as well as a few other things about Clint.

"I haven't owned it long," he said. "But I intend for it to be home."

"Why?" she asked. The log walls and low wood ceiling and hardwood floors made the place seem dark and small. It felt like a sad place to her, sadder even than the shabby apartment she'd shared with her brother.

He shrugged, then flinched. "I like the solitude."

"Then why did you bring *me* here?" she asked, forcing a smile for both their sakes. She wanted to distract him from his pain and herself from her fear.

But maybe there was another way she could distract them...

First, she had to treat his wound.

"Usually you refuse to talk to me," Clint reminded her.

"You probably prefer that to when I have," she said. And her face flushed slightly as she recalled some of the hateful things she'd hurled at him.

He didn't deny it, but his sexy mouth curved into a slight grin. And her heart skipped a beat at the sight of it. He was so damn good-looking, even with that blood on his face. She needed to clean and treat that wound, so he didn't scar.

"Where's the first aid kit?" she asked.

He gestured to the bathroom, and she hurried over to it. The room was bigger than she'd thought it would be, or maybe it only looked that way because it was bright with a wide window high in one of the white beadboard walls. There was enough space for a double vanity, a linen closet and a big claw-foot tub. She gazed wistfully at that tub for a long moment.

"You can use it," Clint said from where he stood in the doorway.

Heat flushed her face that he'd caught her salaciously eyeing a bathtub. "I've just never seen one that big," she murmured. So big that they would both fit in it. And she closed her eyes on that image, of the two of them naked in a tub full of water and bubbles.

Clint groaned.

And she opened her eyes, worried that he was in pain and she was taking so long to help him. His face was flushed, and his green eyes had gone dark. But he didn't look like the pain he was in had anything to do with his injuries.

Had he been imagining the same thing she had? The two of them naked in that tub?

Her hand shaking, she pulled open the linen closet door and reached for the kit, which was on the shelf above a bunch of towels. The towels looked new and soft. She could imagine him wrapping one around her to warm her skin. Or would he do that with his lips?

His mouth…

She turned to find it close to hers, as he'd sat on the counter between the sinks. "You really need to have a doctor look at this," she said.

He shook his head. "You seemed to know more than that resident who stitched me up."

"I've been in the medical field longer than he has," she explained. She'd worked her way through high school and college as a nursing assistant in the ER.

"So you can treat me," he said.

And she couldn't argue with that. She dabbed at the wound with a hydrogen peroxide–soaked cotton ball, cleaning away the blood. It was a shallow cut, not a through-and-through. She released a breath of relief. But she knew that wasn't the only place he'd been hit.

"Take off your shirt," she told him.

He arched his eyebrows. Maybe he was remembering when she'd tried tugging it off in bed at the safe house.

If Parker hadn't called and interrupted them, what would have happened? Would he have stopped when he'd touched her? Or would he have taken off her scrubs top?

Her skin heated and tingled at just the thought of him touching her. But she needed to touch him.

"I need to look at that shoulder wound," she said. "I can tell it's bothering you."

Had the resident ever made it back to fix those sutures? She couldn't remember if he had—before that kid had pulled a knife on her. And Clint had saved her.

He'd saved her at the safe house, too, even though he'd come under attack. He must have been remembering that attack, because he hesitated before removing his holster. And when he did, he kept it next to him on the counter. Then he pulled off his shirt, baring his chest and abdomen.

"Thank you," she murmured.

"For taking off my shirt?"

She was grateful for that and not just so she could look at his wounded shoulder. She was most grateful that he'd saved her life so many times.

"Thank you for protecting me," she said.

"I have my reasons," he said.

And her face flushed with embarrassment. "I know you're just doing your job." And doing it well.

"I promised Javier," he said.

And she looked up at him. "What?"

"He was worried about you," Clint said, "even before…" His voice trailed off as if it was even harder for him to speak of her brother's death than it was for her. And maybe it was, since he blamed himself for it. "He asked me to make sure that you stayed safe."

She sighed. Javier…

He'd been playing matchmaker. He'd always wanted her to find a good guy who could take care of her, so she wouldn't have to work so hard and so many hours.

"That must have been hard for you when I wouldn't let you anywhere near me," she said.

He sighed. "Very hard."

Like his body. The man was all rock-solid muscle. She stepped closer to him, to inspect his shoulder, and she could feel the heat of his chest against her breasts. Once again, the bandage on his shoulder was saturated with blood. But when she peeled it off, the wound looked better than it had that morning. The doctor must have re-sutured it. The blood on the bandage hadn't come from the old wound. There was a new one now, a hole that was no shallow scratch like the one on his cheek.

She gasped. "Clint! You've been shot."

He touched it. "It went through," he said, dismissing the wound.

"And as it was doing that, the bullet could have nicked an artery or a nerve or torn some muscle tissue," she said, panic stealing away her breath and making her heart race. "You need to go to the hospital."

"It's fine," he insisted. "Lucky for me whoever shot me didn't have one of the guns with the special ammo in it. This is nothing."

She shook her head, unable to believe that he was treating a gunshot wound like the scratch on his face. "You must be in incredible pain."

"I am," he said. "But it's not because of that little .22 bullet that went through my shoulder."

"Then I don't—"

His mouth covered hers, cutting off whatever else she'd been about to say. And she couldn't remember when he kissed her, when he touched her.

She couldn't remember that she was supposed to hate him. She knew only that she wanted him every bit as much as he seemed to want her. But he was hurt, and the nurse in her could not ignore that. She pulled back, panting for breath, and asked, "Are you sure you're not hurting?"

"Oh, I am," he said, but his lips curved into a wicked grin. "I'm hurting."

"Stop it!" she admonished him.

And he immediately pulled back. "I'm sorry. I didn't mean to make you uncomfortable. That wasn't…" He pushed a slightly shaking hand through his hair. "I thought you felt it, too."

She groaned with frustration. "That's the problem."

"That you don't?"

"That I do," she admitted. And now she reached for him. He'd said he was fine, so she would take him at his word. And in her opinion, he was very fine—with all that taut muscle and those chiseled good looks.

She pressed her mouth to his, kissing him as hungrily as he'd just kissed her. He tasted so damn good that she moaned. Her lips tingled, her skin heated, and her heart pounded like mad.

She'd never felt this attraction to anyone before. Why this man? Why the man she'd been so convinced that she would hate forever?

Since he was sitting on the counter, she couldn't

get as close as she wanted to be to him. She wanted to press her body against his like she'd pressed her mouth. But only their mouths touched, lips nibbling and clinging to each other's.

Then he slid his tongue between her lips, deepening the kiss. And he tasted her like she'd tasted him. A groan rumbled from his throat.

Suddenly he moved. As he slid off the counter, he scooped her up in his arms.

"Clint!" she protested.

And he stopped, just as he had moments ago. "Did you change your mind?" he asked, his voice gruff with desire and regret.

She'd never made up her mind. Hell, she couldn't think at all—except about him. "You can't carry me," she protested. "You're hurt."

He chuckled—with relief and apparently amusement at her concern—and he continued to carry her despite her protest. He swung her through the bathroom doorway and took her to the bed in the corner of that one-room cabin.

The bed was so big that it dominated the whole space. Like the rest of the cabin, it was made of logs, each of the four posters being thick ones. It was so sturdy that when he laid her on it, it didn't even move. Only the soft mattress shifted beneath her, taking her weight and then his as he followed her down.

Despite his wounded shoulder, he moved quickly. Maybe he was worried that she might change her mind after all. He pulled off her scrub pants and then her shirt. His breath escaped in a gasp as he stared down at her bra and panties.

Her underwear was nothing fancy, nothing expensive, but she'd made it cute when she'd embroidered little roses on the white cotton. She'd done it for herself, to feel pretty. But now, with Clint staring at her so intensely, she felt beautiful and sexy.

"You take my breath away," he murmured, his voice gruff with emotion.

"That's probably the gunshot wound doing that," she said.

He shook his head. "It's you. You are so beautiful." He said it like it frustrated him—just like it frustrated her that she found him so attractive, too attractive to hate the way she wanted to hate him.

But she didn't want to hate him anymore. She just wanted him. So she reached for him, tugging on the waistband of his jeans to bring him closer. Then she undid the button and pulled down the zipper.

And his breath hissed out with the sound of the zipper. "Rosie…"

She stroked her fingers over the erection that pushed against his knit boxers. And he groaned as if he'd been shot again.

Maybe it was her. Thinking that gave her such a sense of power. She watched his reaction to every stroke of her fingers, to her lips sliding over his neck…

And he reacted to every touch, every kiss, until he was panting for breath. Instead of pulling down his boxers and taking her, he gently pushed her back against the pillows. Then he made her as crazy as she'd made him.

He unhooked her bra and dropped it onto the floor. Then he caressed her breasts, moving his fingers gently around and around them until finally he brushed the pad of his thumb across a nipple.

She arched off the mattress and cried out. And a need like she'd never felt before gripped her. Tension wound tightly inside her.

He closed his lips around that taut nipple, and she nearly came at the sensation. But he wasn't done. He pushed her panties down her legs and then he moved his mouth there—to her core. And he made love to her until pleasure overtook her and she found a release.

But it wasn't enough. She wanted more. She wanted to feel him inside her. So she tugged at him again, trying to pull him up her body.

He moved away instead. And she released a little cry of disappointment. But he was only pulling a condom from the pocket of his jeans. He pushed down his boxers and rolled on the condom before he returned to the bed. Then he joined their bodies, easing inside her.

She raised her legs, taking him deeper. And she wrapped her arms around him, clutching him close.

He stared down at her, and there was such intensity in those deep green eyes of his that she nearly shuddered with release just from that look. And he moved, thrusting gently in and out of her.

She met each thrust with an arch of her hips, taking him deeper yet. He fit her so perfectly, as if he'd been made for her or her for him. And what should have felt wrong—so wrong—actually felt right. So very right.

"Clint…" His name escaped her lips on a moan.

He leaned down and brushed his mouth across hers. Then he deepened the kiss. And as he kissed her, he touched her, moving his hand between their bodies. He stroked a nipple and then he trailed his hand lower, to the most sensitive part of her body. As he stroked that, she came with a release so powerful that tears leaked from the corners of her eyes.

Then his body tensed. Maybe he had seen her tears. But then he joined her in pleasure with a long release of his own. Maybe he hadn't seen the tears. He left her—for just a few moments—to use the bathroom. When he returned, he pulled her into his arms. "Are you all right? Did I hurt you?"

He had seen the tears.

She shook her head. But she couldn't speak. She was too overwhelmed with emotion—with embarrassment.

"I'm sorry," he said. "I shouldn't have taken advantage of you."

She laughed now. "I'm not sure who took advantage of whom," she said. "You're the one who's hurt."

"I'm fine," he assured her. "But you must be exhausted. Close your eyes. Rest."

Maybe he was a hypnotist because, despite her concern for him, she did as he said. She closed her eyes. But she wouldn't have believed that she could rest, not with all the emotions and fears running through her. But she felt safe in Clint's arms—safer than she could ever remember feeling. That should have scared her even more than someone wanting her dead.

Clint struggled to awaken, to open his eyes, which were still gritty with sleep. He couldn't remember the last time he'd slept so deeply. Certainly not since Javier had died.

And the dream he'd had…

He jerked awake. That hadn't been a dream. He'd made love with Rosie Mendez. But when he opened his eyes, she was gone. The sheets were tangled around him, around his naked body—which was hard again with wanting her.

And he and the sheets smelled like her, like vanilla and that spice. Maybe cinnamon.

She had been here. It hadn't been just a dream.

But where the hell was she now?

Some damn bodyguard he had proven to be; he'd lost her again. How was he supposed to protect her when he didn't even know where she was?

How could he have fallen asleep? Sure, he'd been exhausted. And so had she. But he wasn't certain that was why she'd cried after they'd made love. Had she been that regretful? Had she felt as if she'd betrayed Javier?

She hated Clint. Why would she have had sex with him? Unless she'd been up to something.

He jumped up from the bed and grabbed his clothes. After dressing, he hurried out to the lean-to where he'd parked the SUV. Had she taken the keys? Was that why she'd slept with him? To disarm him and take off?

But the SUV was there.

If she was gone from the property, she must have left with someone else. But by her own admission, she wasn't close to anyone. Unless she'd lied about that.

But she'd sounded lonely, so he believed she'd been telling the truth. And maybe last night had just been about that loneliness and fear and having to connect with another human being even if that human being was him.

But where was she now? Had someone taken her?

He studied the driveway, trying to tell if there were any other tire tracks on it. He hadn't heard a vehicle drive up, but then he'd apparently been dead to the world because he hadn't felt her leave his arms or the bed.

Where the hell had she gone?

Where the hell had they gone?

"You're sure he was hurt?" he asked.

"There was blood on the sidewalk where he'd pulled the SUV," Nikki said. "And I swear I saw him get hit at least once."

A twinge of pain struck Parker's heart. But he wasn't the only one bothered by the news. Landon Myers looked sick. He and Clint were so close that they shared a house in the city.

Clint hadn't gone there. Landon had already checked. His principal—as the client in a bodyguard assignment was called—sat next to Landon. Jocelyn Gerber looked sick, too.

But she wasn't worried about Clint. She was worried about the witness. "What about Ms. Mendez?" she asked Nikki. "Was she injured?"

Nikki shrugged. "Like I told my brother, the SUV came under heavy fire. She could have been."

Jocelyn gasped. "That is unacceptable. The Payne Protection Agency's main responsibility was to make sure that nothing happened to the witness—"

And Landon lost his temper. "Do your damn job," he said, "and you won't need Rosie's testimony."

"What do you mean?" she asked. "Of course I've done my job."

"Offer those shooters a plea deal to turn on Luther. There are plenty of them in custody thanks to the Payne Protection Agency," Landon said with pride.

"Even you should be able to get through to one of them."

Jocelyn glared at him. "Then I need to go down to the jail," she said as she rose from her chair around the conference table. "We're obviously wasting our time here."

Landon grimaced, and Parker mouthed *I'm sorry* at him. He'd had no idea that Jocelyn Gerber would be so difficult for his friend to handle. Landon got up to follow her out, but he paused at the door and turned back. "Let me know when you find Clint."

"Do you have any ideas?" Parker asked. "He's not answering his phone."

"And I can't even pick up a signal for it," Nikki added.

Landon shook his head and turned back toward the door. But then he stopped and swiveled around. "What about his cabin? Did you check there?"

"What cabin?" Parker had never figured Clint for the outdoors type. All he ever remembered him doing was working—first as a vice cop and now as a bodyguard.

"He just bought the place a little while ago," Landon said.

"He didn't mention it."

Landon grimaced again. "Yeah, he probably wouldn't have said anything about it to you."

Parker felt a pang. And now he knew what his brother Cooper had gone through when he'd become the boss to his friends. It wasn't always easy to maintain friendships when you were suddenly the one in charge. "Why not to me?"

"It's the cabin Cooper owned."

"My brother?" As far as Parker knew, Cooper had never owned a cabin—unless he'd been keeping things from him, too.

"Officer Cooper," Landon said.

The man who'd killed Parker's father. He shuddered. He'd never intended to go back there. Ever.

"He bought it really cheap from the guy's estate, which just recently got settled," Landon said. "It had been in probate for years…"

"Does anyone else know about it?" Parker asked.

Landon shrugged. "I think everybody in vice knew he'd bought it. He was trying to buy it off the estate before it even got settled."

So everybody but Parker knew about it. Of course, Parker had left vice long before these guys had.

"Do you remember where it is?" Landon asked.

Parker nodded. He would never forget. Now he had to go back. He only hoped that when he did, it wouldn't end as it had the last time—in another death.

Chapter 15

Rosie was lost—in more ways than one. When she'd awakened in Clint's arms, that sense of security she'd felt had fled, replaced with a panic more terrifying than any she'd experienced before. She'd needed to get away from him. So she'd carefully extricated herself from his grasp, causing him to murmur in protest in his sleep.

Then she'd slid out of the bed and had quickly dressed in her scrubs again. But the cabin was so small that she hadn't been able to get far enough away from him—and not still want him. She'd wanted to crawl back into bed with him, back into his arms.

She'd wanted to wake him with kisses and caresses, with her body sliding over his hard, muscular one. Heat flashed through her at the thought, warming the chill from her skin.

It was cold outside. When she'd stepped out of the cabin earlier, the cool air had felt good against her heated skin. But now…

The cold had seeped deeper into her flesh. She wore only her scrubs. She'd left the borrowed parka at the hospital yesterday, but she wished she had it now. The early-morning air was colder here. They must have been near a lake, because it was damp, too.

She shivered. She needed to head back toward the cabin. But as she turned in a circle in that heavily wooded area, nothing looked familiar. She wasn't sure from which direction she had come.

She shouldn't have wandered off on her own. But she'd needed to get away from Clint. She'd needed to think…

About him.

About last night.

About Javier.

Had she betrayed her brother? Or had she done exactly what he'd wanted?

She shivered again. For so long she'd thought that Javier had been wrong to idolize Clint, to trust him. And she'd thought that she would never be able to trust him. Despite her resentment of him, she had started to, though.

Had that been a mistake? Had it all been a mistake?

Not that he'd taken advantage of her like he'd lamented. As she'd told him, she wasn't sure who'd taken advantage of whom. He was wounded—in pain.

Was he thinking any clearer than she was?

If he had been, certainly he would know that they had no future. But maybe he was one of those guys who preferred one-night stands to relationships.

That was all last night had been.

One night.

It could never happen again. They could never have a relationship.

A pang of regret struck her. But that wasn't because of the relationship.

It couldn't be.

It was because of last night. Because she never should have had sex with him.

Now it was all she could think about—all she wanted. Him.

Had he awakened yet? Would he find her?

Because she was certainly lost. What was a lost person supposed to do? Sit down and wait to be found?

She remembered all those stories about people getting lost on hikes and how they'd wandered farther away from the trail than they'd thought.

And Rosie—who was used to city streets and sidewalks—hadn't understood how that was possible. How could a person walk farther than they'd realized? Wouldn't they feel it?

She hadn't. She had been so preoccupied with thoughts of last night, with thoughts of Clint, that she had no idea how long or far she'd walked.

She could have been miles from the cabin or just around the corner. And it was that possibility that she might be closer than she thought that compelled her to walk just a little farther. Maybe she would be able to see the roof of the cabin through the trees. But instead she saw a glint of water through them, and then she realized the noise she'd been hearing had been the rush of water moving over the rocks in the riverbed. She walked closer to it.

Wasn't that a way to get unlost? Follow a river to civilization?

She had no idea how far away civilization might be, though. Certainly they hadn't driven that far from River City last night. Not that River City was exactly civilized. Even now, after new leadership had been brought in to clean up the corruption in the police department, there was a leak in it and in the district attorney's office.

And those leaks reported to Luther Mills.

Maybe there were leaks within the Payne Protection Agency, too—since both Parker Payne and Detective Dubridge had ordered Clint to take her back to the safe house. Had one of them set up that ambush?

Clint was friends with both of those men. Had he told them about his cabin? Did anyone know about it?

Another chill rushed through her, and it had nothing to do with the early-morning air now and everything to do with fear. Maybe she didn't want to be found— if whoever found her might be working for Luther.

Something snapped. Loud. It had to be, for her to have heard it over the rush of the river.

And it was close, too.

Then something else snapped. Twigs? Branches?

Someone had found her. Rosie just wasn't sure who or what it was.

Clint knew Rosie was a city girl. He'd seen her uneasiness with the area when he'd pulled up to the cabin the evening before. There was no way she'd wandered off in the woods. She'd probably gone looking for the street instead.

So he walked down the muddy drive toward the

street. As he drew closer, he noticed a glint through the trees. It wasn't off asphalt. The road was more gravel and dirt than anything else. It was off metal.

He drew his weapon. And as he stepped closer, he identified the glint as belonging to vehicles. Two pickups were parked alongside the road, teetering precariously on the edge of those deep ditches.

They'd been parked there in a hurry. Then he noticed the trail going from them, down through the brush and weeds. Had they seen something?

Someone?

Were they even now chasing Rosie down?

He cursed himself for falling asleep. His job was to protect her. But protecting Rosie was more than an assignment to him; he'd made a promise to her brother.

And now he might have failed him.

Grasping his weapon tightly, he headed down that makeshift trail through the woods. It came close to the cabin. If Rosie had been running near it, why hadn't she screamed for him, for help?

Maybe those vehicles had nothing to do with her. It wasn't as if anyone would have known where to find him.

Sure, he'd told some people in the vice unit about trying to buy the place, but only one knew that the sale had finally closed. Landon...

Had his roommate told his principal? Had he mentioned anything to Jocelyn Gerber?

Clint worried that he might have. And he, for one, did not trust the assistant district attorney at all. She could have told Luther.

Hell, she might have even been able to find out

about it without Landon mentioning anything. The sale had been a matter of public record.

Nikki Payne wasn't the only one who could find anything online. Other people could as well.

Maybe bringing Rosie here had been a bad idea. It had given him a false sense of security, so much so that he'd fallen asleep. So much so that he'd crossed the line with his client.

He shouldn't have made love with her. If he hadn't, he probably wouldn't have fallen asleep. He would have been as tense and frustrated as he'd been the night before. And if he hadn't, Rosie might not have taken off on her own.

It must have rattled her so much that she'd wanted to escape him. He'd seen those tears she'd shed after.

It had affected her.

And it had affected him as well. He'd never experienced anything as powerful as that. But he didn't expect to experience it again—even if he found her.

Where the hell was she?

He thought about calling out for her. But he didn't want to alert anyone else to his presence. They weren't alone in the woods. And since there had been two trucks parked beside the road, there were at least two possible shooters.

Maybe more.

He'd survived the attack the night before only because he hadn't been alone. If there hadn't been so many other bodyguards, he had no doubt that he would have died, and Rosie as well.

No. Taking her off alone had been a very bad idea.

He hurried forward along the path, but he was careful to make as little noise as possible. But someone else wasn't being as cautious.

He heard twigs or branches snapping. Then he heard something else, something that chilled his blood and had his heart racing.

Rosie's scream. Her voice was high and sharp and full of fear.

As with the television room, Luther had unlimited access to the weight room. But no matter how many weights he lifted, he couldn't get the pressure off his chest.

For the first time since he'd put those bullets in Javier Mendez, he was worried that he might actually go to prison for the damn kid's murder.

That wasn't possible, though.

He'd committed so many other crimes and hadn't even been prosecuted. He was untouchable.

Or he had been until that damn Payne Protection Agency had gotten involved. What the hell was the deal with those bodyguards? They'd taken out a few of Luther's crew. It had been his guys in those body bags he'd seen on the news. And another had died at the hospital. In addition to the casualties, Payne Protection bodyguards had overpowered several more of Luther's crews and turned them over to the police, who had them into custody.

He'd seen a few of them at the jail. They'd looked scared. Maybe too scared...

And then that damn ADA had started calling them down to the visiting rooms to talk to them. Probably to offer them deals to turn on him.

He hurled the weights, instead of lifting them. They

went only so far before they dropped and clunked against the concrete floor.

Jocelyn Gerber was wasting her time, though. His guys would not talk to her. He'd already warned them that whoever did would die—slowly, painfully.

And their families would, too.

Nobody would dare betray him.

But then he hadn't really thought Rosie would talk, either. He'd thought that she would have learned her lesson from what he'd done to her rat of a little brother. Now he'd have to do that to her—put some bullets in her.

He would just have to get someone to do it who was up to the job, unlike all those damn flunkies he'd sent after her. This time he would not fail to eliminate the witness.

Chapter 16

Rosie's lungs burned with fear and exertion. She had never run as fast as she was now, not even when the ER had been at its busiest. But then she'd never had to run for her life before like she was now.

She had never seen anything as big or as fearsome as the monster she'd glimpsed through the trees. And the minute she'd seen it, that bloodcurdling scream had torn its way out of her throat.

So then it had seen her.

So screaming had been stupid.

And so was running.

From the nature survival shows Javier had watched, she knew she was supposed to lie down and play like she was dead so that it wouldn't chase her. It wasn't as if she could actually outrun a bear.

And that thing…

It must have been a bear. But it hadn't looked like

the ones she'd seen on TV. Its fur had been matted with burrs and buzzing with flies. It hadn't looked regal or beautiful. It had looked like a beast.

And it was probably running her down right now to eat her. So she forced her feet to move. It was too late to lie down and play dead. And she was afraid that if she did that, the act would become real all too soon anyway.

Thorns clutched at her scrubs, tearing through the thin material. But worse than that, the bushes caught and held her, slowing her down until she managed to break away. She'd lost too much time, though.

She could hear it closing in on her, could hear branches snapping and breaking beneath its weight as it pursued her. Then another branch caught her, this one wrapping around her ankle, and she crashed to the ground.

She kicked out, trying to fight free of the tendrils of that thorn bush. But the thorns caught her skin, digging deep. She couldn't escape.

And then she was suddenly plunged into the darkness of the big shadow looming over her.

And she screamed again.

Rosie's scream squeezed Clint's heart in a tight vise. He leaned down and pushed her hair back from her face, but she flinched as if she'd thought he would strike her.

"Rosie, it's me." She wasn't afraid of *him*, was she?

Because even after he identified himself, she kept trembling. She was still so scared. She pressed her hands against the ground and pushed herself up. And she seemed about to take off running again. But she reached out a muddy hand toward him, to pull him along with her. "We have to get out of here!"

Now her fear was his. His hand was already on his holster, but now he pulled his weapon. "Why?" he asked. "Did you see someone?"

Maybe the people from the truck had tracked her down, but she'd gotten away from them. She was strong and smart and resourceful.

She shook her head, and she looked all wild-eyed. "No. Not a human."

Clint furrowed his brow as confusion gripped him. "Then what the hell was it?"

"A bear," she said, and she glanced fearfully around them.

"I didn't see anything," he said, trying to reassure her.

But she shook her head again. "I did," she said. "I saw him back there…" She gestured a shaking hand toward one section of the woods. Then she pointed in another direction. "Or maybe there…"

"I didn't see anything," he told her again.

She narrowed her eyes and glared at him. "Are you telling me that I just imagined seeing that—that thing?"

He believed she'd definitely seen something. She was still trembling with fear. He wanted her to relax now, though, so he teased, "I'm telling you that your screaming probably scared him away."

She shuddered. "I thought you were the bear when you were standing over me." She blinked hard as if fighting back tears. "I thought I was going to die. I know I probably came closer before—at my apartment and the hospital and…" She gestured at his shoulder.

"And when you were shot. But I think I'd rather get shot than eaten by a bear." She shuddered again.

And he couldn't blame her. While he hadn't seen the animal, she had definitely seen one. He'd heard rumors about black bear sightings in the area. He shivered now, thinking of how she might have been attacked.

He reached out and pulled her trembling body into his arms. At first she tensed up, as if she didn't want him touching her. Then she clutched his T-shirt in her hands and snuggled even closer to him. "You're safe," he assured her. "Nothing's going to happen to you."

Not while he was alive.

Her breath escaped in a shaky sigh. Maybe she believed him.

But he couldn't protect her if she kept taking off on him. "What the hell were you doing all the way out here?" he asked. And he ran his hands over her back. She was cold, too.

"I told you—I was running from the bear." She pulled away from him now and wrapped her arms around herself, as if unwilling to accept his comfort.

"Why were you outside?" he asked. "Were you trying to get away from me?"

Her face flushed, and it wasn't from her run through the woods. She wouldn't meet his gaze, either.

"What the hell were you thinking, Rosie?" he asked. "You know you need protection. Luther is determined to have you killed. Why would you take off on your own?"

"I wasn't leaving," she said. "I just wanted some air. You told me we were safe here."

That was what he'd thought, too. But then he remembered the trucks parked on the side of the road. And he wondered if they would be safe anywhere.

"What?" she asked. "What is it?"

She must have seen the worry on his face. That was why Landon liked playing cards with him. Clint had no poker face; he couldn't bluff.

"We need to get back to the cabin," he said. Actually, they needed to get back to the SUV and get the hell out of there.

She glanced around the woods, her eyes wild. "Did you hear the bear?" she asked anxiously. "Is it back?"

"I'm not worried about the bear."

"But you're worried," she said.

He didn't want to scare her any more than she already was.

"Tell me why," she implored him. "I hate secrets."

He was already keeping one from her—Javier's reason for becoming his informant. But he couldn't burden her with the guilt of that, of her brother wanting to regain her respect. "I saw two trucks out by the road."

Her eyes widened. "You think someone found us?"

He shrugged. "I don't know why else they'd be here."

His was the only cabin for miles.

She spun around in a circle again. "Then we shouldn't go back to the cabin. They could be waiting for us there."

They could. She had a valid point.

"There's no way we can get that far from them on foot," he pointed out, especially with bears in the woods as well. But he didn't want to remind her of that animal she'd seen. "We need the vehicle."

She nodded. "Okay." She stared at the trees all

around them. "I hope you know where the hell it is, because I have no idea."

He chuckled. "You're no survivalist, huh?"

She shook her head. "No, that was Javier. He loved those shows." She uttered a shaky sigh. "Maybe he could have survived out here better than he had on the streets."

Clint had bought the cabin because of her brother. Javier had talked often about wanting to learn to fish and hunt; he would have loved the place. If only Clint could have closed on the purchase of it before Javier had been murdered.

The guilt gripped him, weighing heavily on his shoulders. "It's this way," he told her, but as he moved through the trees, a low branch scraped over his shoulder. A curse slipped through his lips at the pain.

"You need—"

"I know," he interrupted, and finished for her, "medical attention." He'd rather have hers. But he could guess why she'd gone off alone in the woods. It hadn't been to get away from the cabin; it had been to get away from him.

She grabbed his arm, her fingers squeezing. Maybe she just didn't want to get separated from him and lost.

Or maybe she thought she'd heard the bear again. Clint heard something, too. But it wasn't the sound of anything or anyone moving through the brush.

It was the metallic click of a gun cocking. And his was still in his holster.

Damn it!

The men from the truck had found them, and they were armed. Before he could react, shots rang out.

* * *

Woodrow had thought his years as a bureau chief for the FBI had been stressful. Taking this position with the River City Police Department would be almost like taking early retirement.

But this new job was a hell of a lot more stressful than any position he'd previously held. He hated that he couldn't trust his own damn officers. He'd been able to trust his agents. And because he wasn't able to trust his officers, he'd had to enlist people he had faith in to help him.

But now those people were in danger because they were helping him. And they were family.

He could see the concern in his wife, in the way her brow furrowed with worry, in the tension in her petite body. She often visited him at the River City PD to bring him coffee or cookies or just to give him a kiss and a shoulder rub. But he knew she had another reason for coming by his office today.

She was having one of her notorious premonitions. She didn't even need to tell him.

"I'm sorry," he told her. "I shouldn't have brought the Payne Protection Agency into this."

What the hell was this? It felt like war; it was certainly beginning to rack up casualties like war.

Nikki could have been shot the night before when all those bullets had been flying. Instead she'd taken out one of the gunmen.

Penny came around his desk and pushed him and his chair back. Then she settled onto his lap and wrapped her arm around his neck. "You had to," she said. "You need protection for everyone involved in this trial. And there is nobody better at security than the Payne Protection Agency."

"That's true," he agreed. "They are the best." He rubbed his fingers over the furrow in her brow. "So you don't need to worry…"

But she would—just like he was worrying.

"I'm a mother," she said. "It's what I do."

But she didn't worry only about her own kids. She worried about every one of those bodyguards just like they were hers. And they were. But they weren't just hers now. They were his, too.

She pressed a kiss to his cheek. "You're worried, too."

He nodded. Then he summoned the courage and asked, "Who is it?"

"What?"

"Who did you have the premonition about?" he asked. "Who's in danger now?"

She shuddered as the feeling overwhelmed her.

He could feel it, too, the fear and the dread. They were so attuned to each other. He'd never had a connection with another human being like he had with Penny. She was more than his wife. She was his soul mate.

"Who?" he persisted.

She clearly didn't want to tell him, so it was someone he knew, someone he loved.

"Gage?"

His son-in-law worked for Logan's team, but this assignment was so big Parker had brought in his brothers' agencies for support. His daughter Megan had thought she'd lost Gage once, when he'd gone missing in action during a deployment. She couldn't lose him again.

Penny shook her head, tousling her short auburn curls around her beautiful face. "No."

"Nick?" Woodrow had a special bond with his former agent. He had always been like a son to him. But he'd actually been Penny's late husband's son.

Her breath escaped in a shaky sigh, and on that sigh, she whispered a name. "Parker."

And he knew that her feeling was strong. Parker was in danger. And it was all Woodrow's fault for giving him the assignment.

"He would have been hurt if you hadn't given it to him," Penny said, as if she'd read his mind. And maybe she had. "This is personal to him. Luther Mills was always the one that got away from him. You've given him the chance to change that."

But Parker's situation was different now. He wasn't the young vice cop going after the drug dealer. He was a man with a wife and with children. This assignment could not cost him that.

It could not cost him his life.

Chapter 17

Rosie held her breath, waiting for the bullets to strike her as they had Clint back at the safe house. But his body covered hers. If any shots came near them, the bullets would strike him first.

Again.

But while the gun blasts were loud, there was no rustle of bullets moving through the brush or trees around them. Whoever was shooting was shooting away from them, not toward them.

Then the gunfire abruptly stopped, and voice called out, "Oh my God, we didn't see you. Are you all right?"

Clint didn't move off her immediately. Had he been hit?

The man who'd spoken must have thought so, because he cursed. But he was cursing himself. "Oh God, I hit you. You're bleeding!"

Clint moved then, but he moved slowly to his feet. Then he reached down to help her up, but as he did, he stepped between her and the man speaking to them. "I'm fine," he told the guy. But then he tensed as a couple more men joined the first one.

They were all older guys, probably in their sixties or early seventies. So it was unlikely they were working for Luther. They carried weapons, but they were also wearing orange vests and hats. They must have just been hunting.

"But you're bleeding," the first man said. "I must have hit you."

Clint shook his head. "This is an old injury."

"Can't be that old," the hunter said, "since it's still bleeding."

"He needs stitches," Rosie said.

The guy angled his head to peer around Clint, who blocked her with his body. "You a nurse? I don't remember any clinics or doctor offices in this area."

"I work at—"

"In the city," Clint interrupted, and spoke for her.

Rosie would have bristled with indignation. But she realized that despite their ages and attire, Clint didn't trust these guys.

"Hey, you look familiar," one of the other men remarked.

And Rosie ducked farther behind Clint now. Maybe he had a good reason to mistrust them.

"You with the River City PD?" the guy asked Clint.

Clint shook his head.

"Sure you were," the guy persisted. "Vice unit, right?"

"You're a police officer?" Clint asked him, without answering his question.

The guy chuckled. "Not for a few years. I earned my retirement. But once a cop always a cop, right?"

Clint shook his head again.

Why had Clint quit the force at such a young age? Did his guilt over Javier's death have anything to do with it?

Rosie felt a pang of regret for adding to his guilt with all her recriminations. But it had been his fault, right? For forcing Javier to become an informant...

But had he forced Javier?

Her brother was headstrong—like her. If he hadn't wanted to help Clint, he would have refused. And maybe he'd even liked helping him.

She suppressed a sigh.

"I could swear you worked vice with the Myers kid and that little girl..."

A muscle twitched in Clint's cheek as he clenched his jaw. Did he want to defend his friend? But he refrained.

And Rosie couldn't help but wonder again if the blonde was just a friend to Clint. She'd certainly come quickly to his defense the day before in the locker room.

Another of the men uttered a low whistle of appreciation. "She was a cute little thing," he remarked. "Great bait for johns..."

Rosie cleared her throat, reminding them that there was a woman present—one who didn't appreciate women being referred to as cute little things.

The guy's face flushed, and he changed the subject. "You sure you didn't get shot? We all got a little car-

ried away when we saw the buck—had to be at least
an eight-point."

Deer hunters. That was what they were.

Another of the guys snorted. "Maybe six."

"Bernie's like this when we go fishing, too," the
first man remarked. "Exaggerates the size of every
damn fish that got away from him."

"Well, we'll let you get back to your hunting," Clint
said, and he closed his hand around Rosie's wrist to
guide her from the woods. But he hesitated when the
men did not move.

"What are you doing out here?" one of the men
asked with suspicion in his voice. "Doesn't look like
either of you is dressed for hunting."

Clint moved his hand from her wrist to entwine
their fingers. His mouth moved into a smile, but it
didn't warm the intensity in his green eyes. "Just out
for a short hike before she heads to work."

"It's dangerous walking in the woods during hunting season, especially without wearing any bright
clothes," one of the men chimed in. "You could have
been shot."

Rosie wasn't entirely certain that Clint hadn't been.
And if he had been, she wasn't entirely certain that it
had been an accident.

There was something slightly off about these guys.
The chief had admitted to having a leak in his department. That leak could have extended to retired officers.

The same thing must have occurred to Clint, because he seemed anxious to get away from them.
"We're going to take your advice," he said, "and get
the hell out of here."

But when he stepped forward, the man didn't move.

And fear gripped Rosie again. While they were older men, there were three of them and only one of Clint. And he was injured…

As they headed through the woods, Clint felt a tingling between his shoulder blades—like someone was watching him. The hunters?

He'd had a weird feeling about them, especially since they'd acted as if they'd recognized him. Was that just because they had actually worked with him? Or had they been sent after him and Rosie?

But then why had they let them past? It had taken a few seconds—tense seconds—for them to step aside and allow them to pass. But they had allowed them. And if they'd wanted to kill them, certainly they would have just started firing.

All three of them had been armed.

Rosie must have felt the same sensation he had, that they were being watched, because she kept glancing fearfully behind them. "They couldn't work for Luther, could they?" she asked.

He shrugged, then grimaced. His shoulder had taken a hell of a beating the past couple of days. It throbbed, and his shirt was sticky with the blood the guys had seen on him. Knocking Rosie to the ground must have opened his stitches.

"Usually Luther's crew is so young."

But that was only because most of Luther's crew didn't live much beyond their teens. Like Javier, who'd just turned twenty when he was killed.

"But I guess…" she continued.

"Shh," he cautioned. He wanted to listen to see if

the guys were following them. And if they were, he didn't want them to overhear them wondering if they were on Luther Mills's payroll.

"Do you hear something?" she asked.

"Not with your chattering," he remarked.

And she sucked in a breath.

"I'm sorry," he said. He hadn't meant to hurt her feelings. He'd noticed she only talked a lot when she was nervous.

But now she fell silent and remained so until the cabin came into view. Then she said, "I walked behind it. How come we're coming up to it from the front? Was I that lost?"

"No," he assured her. "I didn't want those guys following us back here."

"You think they were following us?" She shivered despite the sun shining brightly around the cabin. "Then they must work for Luther."

"Or they wondered what the hell we were really doing out in the middle of the woods," he said. Just because they were retired didn't mean the ex-officers had lost their lawmen instincts.

He would have been suspicious had he happened upon a couple like him and Rosie in the woods. She'd obviously been frightened. Maybe they'd thought Clint was holding her against her will.

He wanted to hold her again. But he wanted her to be willing. And he doubted that would happen again.

He wasn't sure why she had let him touch her the night before. Maybe she'd just needed something to distract her from the danger she was in.

But there was no escaping it.

He cursed.

And she tensed. "What? Did they follow us?"

Nobody had followed them. But he noticed another vehicle parked out by the road; this one had pulled onto the driveway because he could see the sun glinting off the metallic grille of it.

He pulled the keys from his pocket and handed them to her. He'd found them inside the SUV when he'd been searching for her earlier. If she'd wanted to get away from him, she easily could have. "Go," he told her. "Get in the SUV."

"What—where are you going?" she asked.

"We have company." He glimpsed a shadow passing behind one of the cabin windows. And he ducked behind a tree, tugging Rosie along with him.

"Who is it?" she asked.

"I don't know, but I'm going to find out." And he drew his gun from his holster.

"Just come with me," she urged him. "Let's get out of here."

He wasn't sure that they would be able to, with the other vehicle parked on the driveway, which was really more like a narrow path between the trees. Would there be enough room for the SUV to get past it?

He hoped there was. "If you hear gunfire or anything, take off," he told her. "And if you can't get past that vehicle, just ram it until you have enough room. The SUV has reinforced bumpers and metal."

But last night, and the broken windshield, proved that it wasn't a tank, and they might need one of those to escape if there were more gunmen than there had been at the safe house.

"I don't want to leave you," she said.

"You had no problem doing that this morning," he reminded her.

And her face flushed with color. "Clint—"

"I'm just your bodyguard," he said. "I get that." That last night hadn't meant anything to her. "And you need to understand that my job is to protect you."

"So drive me out of here," she said.

She was right. He should. But he was too curious to find out who was moving around his cabin, the place he'd intended to make his home.

Had one of those guys known where they were going and beaten them back here?

It was possible. Despite their ages, they'd been in good shape, and they'd seemed familiar with the woods. They'd probably been friends of Robert Cooper's. That was why they hunted near his old cabin.

They might have even heard that he'd been trying to buy it from the estate and had known where to find him. He couldn't trust them.

Hell, he couldn't trust anyone right now, not with Rosie's life at stake.

"Your job is to make sure I testify," she reminded him. "You won't be able to do that if you're dead."

He stared at the cabin, though, wanting to know who'd invaded his privacy—his life.

"You don't know how many guys are in there," she said. "You could be walking into a trap."

He could. Was that a chance he was willing to take? If he had only himself to worry about, he would have, gladly.

But he'd promised Javier that he would take care

of Rosie. Yet her brother—of all people—should have known how strong and stubborn Rosie was. She could take care of herself.

Parker couldn't tell if he'd found the right place. There was no address. No vehicle even parked outside, although there had been tracks along the driveway. There'd also been two trucks parked on the road nearby, so the tracks could have come from one of those vehicles. But if so, why hadn't they parked in the driveway?

Why park alongside the ditch as they had?

Because they hadn't wanted Clint to see them approaching the cabin?

If they were here to take out the witness, Clint was outnumbered. That was why Parker didn't wait for backup like his brother Logan had asked.

Logan was close but not close enough to help Clint if he needed it. Parker was. So he'd jumped out of his vehicle and hurried up to the cabin. But if Clint was here, where was the SUV?

Had he ditched it somewhere?

Maybe he thought it had GPS, so it could be located. And he obviously hadn't wanted to be found. Parker walked softly across the porch to the front door. It wasn't locked. It wasn't even completely closed.

Someone had been here.

He pushed open the door and, with his gun drawn, walked inside the cabin. The space was so small that it was easy to see it was empty. The bathroom was empty, too.

He holstered his gun and took his time looking around the cabin. Someone had slept in the bed, but he didn't know who. There were no pictures, was nothing personal in the space.

But there was blood on the sheets near one of the pillows. Whoever had spent the night had been bleeding.

Nikki thought Clint had been hit. How badly?

And where the hell were he and Rosie?

Had she been hit, too?

They damn well could not lose the witness for Luther's trial. Parker had to find her and Clint, had to make sure they were okay. But before he could move toward the door, he heard something.

It wasn't the door creaking.

It was the click of a gun cocking. And he felt the cold steel of the barrel press against the base of his skull. He didn't dare try to draw his gun. Hell, he didn't dare move. One twitch of the finger on the trigger and he'd be dead—killed execution style.

Years ago he'd survived a professional hit that had been put out on him. Some of the most notorious hit men in the country had tried to take him out. But none of them had come as close as whoever had that gun pressed against his head.

Back then he hadn't had much to lose if someone had killed him. Now he had everything. He had Sharon and their family and his own damn business.

He wasn't going down without one hell of a fight.

Chapter 18

She was supposed to be in the SUV, driving herself off to safety. But Rosie grasped the keys in her hand. She hadn't even walked toward the lean-to where Clint had hidden the vehicle. Instead she'd waited just a few seconds before following him into the cabin.

And as she walked into the melee of two men rolling around on the hardwood floor, arms and legs flailing, she screamed. Then she reached for the weapon that must have been knocked from Clint's grasp.

Her hands were shaking so badly, and the gun was so heavy, that she had to grasp it in both hands. She had never held a gun before, let alone fired one. She didn't know where the safety was. If it had been released or not, but she bluffed. "I'll shoot. Stop! I'll shoot!"

"You'd have to take off the safety first," Clint said as he rolled away from the other man. Then he turned toward his boss. "You're damn lucky I had it on or I might have blown your head off when you attacked me."

Parker cursed as he jumped to his feet. "I didn't know it was you."

"Sure, it's my cabin," Clint said as he moved more slowly to his feet. "Who else would it have been?"

Was Clint suspicious of his boss? Did he think Luther had gotten to him? He must have or why else had he pulled his gun on him?

Rosie wondered, too, and she held tightly to the gun yet. Where was the safety? Could she slide it off in time to protect Clint from the man he'd once considered a friend?

But before she could figure it out, Clint took the weapon from her grasp. "Thanks for the backup, Dirty Harriet," he told her. "But you were supposed to be in the SUV."

And it was clear that he wished she was there now as he stepped between her and his boss.

Parker's eyes narrowed at the gesture. "I didn't know it was you when I knocked down the gun," he insisted. "Why the hell did you pull it on me anyway? Couldn't you tell it was me?"

Clint shook his head. "Not in this dim light—with your back to me."

Parker must not have recognized Clint either because he hadn't knocked down just the gun. He must have knocked down Clint, too. There was blood smeared across the hardwood floor where they'd been rolling around, and that blood was trailing down from Clint's shoulder to drip from his fingertips.

She gasped and ran for the first aid kit in the bathroom. She hurried back with the bandages she found. "Take off your shirt," she said.

But he could barely drag it over his head. She had to help. When she saw the wound, she gasped again. Just as she'd thought, he'd ripped the sutures loose. "You need more stitches," she said.

"What the hell happened?" Parker asked.

And she turned to glare at him. "You ripped open the stitches!"

Clint shook his head. "It was already bleeding in the woods—when those hunters started shooting."

And he'd pushed her to the ground to protect her.

"Were you shot again?" she asked. But she saw only the one hole from the night before. That wound looked red and inflamed, though it wasn't bleeding like the cut from the dumpster.

At least he'd had antibiotics at the hospital, so it hadn't gotten infected. Yet.

She pressed the bandages to it and taped them on. But her hands were shaking as she did it. She didn't want to hurt him any more. She didn't want him hurt although she'd once wished him dead—to his face— when he'd shown up at Javier's funeral.

"You were shot last night?" Parker asked. "Nikki thought so."

"What the hell happened last night?" Clint asked. "You assured me it was safe to take Rosie back there. Was it a setup?"

Parker sucked in a breath like Clint had struck him again. "You think I set that up? My sister was there. She was nearly shot. And my team and my friends…"

Clint uttered a ragged sigh. "I'm sorry, man, but

Luther seems capable of getting to anyone. And he must have gotten to someone."

"Not one of my team," Parker insisted. "We're friends. We have one another's backs. I'd trust every one of you with my life."

Even after Clint had nearly taken his?

"So you can trust one of them with Rosie's protection," Parker continued.

Clint shook his head. "Hell, no."

"We need to get her someplace safe," Parker said.

Clint cursed, but he didn't argue. He was obviously still suspicious of the hunters, and now he shared those suspicions with Parker.

"I saw the trucks," his boss said. "That's why I came inside and tried to figure out where the hell you two were." He glanced from one to the other of them.

And Rosie wondered how much he'd figured out. Did he know that they'd shared that bed last night?

Probably. Neither she nor Clint had made the bed. The sheets were tangled; the pillows both bore indents. It was clear they'd both slept in that bed the night before.

Heat rushed to her face.

"Rosie needed to clear her head," Clint said, making it sound as if he'd gone off with her into the woods.

Maybe he didn't want his boss to know she'd slipped away from him.

"We need to take her to another safe house," Parker said. "Right away."

Clint narrowed his eyes.

"It's a condo in Grand Haven that's not far from here," Parker said. "We don't use it that often, so it's safe. Logan was going to stop there and open it up before meeting me here."

Rosie wanted to stay here—at the cabin with Clint—where for a brief time she'd felt safe in his arms. But he was hurt. His tussle with his boss had his shoulder bleeding profusely now. He needed medical attention maybe even more than she needed him.

But she did need him.

And that need scared her more than Luther Mills trying to kill her.

"Clint needs to go to the hospital," she said. "Now." Blood was already seeping through the bandage she'd applied.

"There's a hospital in Grand Haven," Parker said. "I'll take Clint there once Logan gets here to take you to the safe house."

She shivered, her blood chilling at the thought of trusting anyone besides Clint, which was ironic considering not long ago he was the last person she would have thought herself capable of trusting.

"Who's Logan?" she asked.

"My brother," Parker said. "My twin, actually. He started the Payne Protection Agency. He's the best. But I'll deny it if you tell him I said that."

He'd probably meant to make her laugh. But Rosie could find nothing funny in her current situation.

The grin slid away from Parker's face, and he turned to Clint. "Logan should be here soon. So we should get ready to leave."

Clint pulled open a dresser drawer and tugged out a shirt. But he grimaced when he tried to get it over his head. Rosie helped, her fingers skimming over his skin, which was warm to her touch. Maybe he was getting infected despite those antibiotics.

Or maybe he was affected by her touch, because when she met his gaze, she saw that his eyes had dilated, the pupils swallowing the deep green. And her breath caught as awareness and desire gripped her.

She wanted him. She shouldn't.

But she couldn't help it, especially after last night. Now she knew how amazing he could make her feel, how much pleasure he could give her.

Maybe it was good if he were no longer her bodyguard. Her life might not be safer with someone else, but her heart certainly would be.

As Clint watched the SUV drive off with Rosie in the passenger seat, he had a sinking feeling in his gut—a sick foreboding that he would never see her again.

"Forget about the hospital," he told Parker. "Let's follow them for backup."

His boss shook his head. "Hell, no. I'm not crossing her. She wants you to go to the hospital."

"She always does," he grumbled.

"Because your shoulder is a mess," Parker said. "You need to get it stitched back up."

That was the least of his concerns at the moment. "Logan alone isn't enough to protect her," he protested.

"And you are?"

"Apparently so," Clint replied defensively. "She's not dead yet."

But he had lost her a couple of times—something he wasn't willing to admit to his boss. Spencer Dubridge had probably informed him, though. Clint had a bad feeling that he was about to lose her again, and that this time would be for good.

"No, she's not," Parker said. "But you had help last night."

He sighed. It was true. Without the other body-guards, he'd have a hell of a lot more than a hole in his shoulder.

"C'mon," Parker said as he headed down the drive-way toward the SUV. "Get in."

But Clint was heading the other way, to the SUV he'd parked in the lean-to.

"Where the hell are you going?" Parker yelled at him.

He jangled the keys that Rosie had handed back to him. "I'm following Logan."

"You're not following Logan unless he lets you," Parker warned him.

When Parker had hired him, he'd given him a brief history of the Payne Protection Agency. He knew that Logan had taught him how to lose a tail. The only person who might have been better at it was Logan's brother-in-law and former criminal Garek Kozminski.

"And he's not going to let you," Parker continued. "And neither am I. Get your ass in my SUV, so I can take you to the damn hospital."

Clint turned back to glare at his boss and just as he did, he noticed a glint between the trees on the side of the driveway. He dived at his friend, knocking him to the ground.

"Son of a bitch!" Parker yelled. "I'm not fighting with you—" He tried to push Clint off.

But Clint held fast to him. "Stay down. Shooter."

And just as he said it, the shots rang out, striking the ground near them and pinging off the side of the SUV.

The gunfire came from more than one direction. But of course; Luther never sent just one shooter. Clint and Parker were surrounded and pinned to the ground.

And Clint realized the reason he'd had that premonition. He wouldn't see Rosie again, but it wasn't because she was going to die.

It was because he was going to.

This was it. Luther just knew, when the smuggled cell phone began to ring, that this was the call he'd been waiting for. "Yes?" he answered, and he was already smiling in anticipation.

He had her now, thanks to Clint Quarters. Had the ex-cop really thought Luther wouldn't find out about his little cabin? Luther shuddered at the idea of living out in the woods.

Who would willingly do something like that?

It sounded worse than jail to Luther. At least here he had access to whatever he wanted. In the woods he'd be too far from fast food and television and phone reception. Right now he heard nothing but static from the other end.

"Hello?" he called out. "I can't hear you."

Then he tensed. It wasn't Clint Quarters calling him again, was it? If so, the guy was like a damn cat. But eventually, even a cat's nine lives ran out.

Clint's would, too.

"Boss?" a voice asked, like he was having as much trouble hearing Luther as Luther was hearing him.

"Yes!" he shouted back. He knew it wasn't Clint.

That stubborn lawman never would have called him boss. "Is it over?" he asked. "Did you get her?"

He must have lost reception again, because there was another long pause.

"Are you there?" he impatiently asked. "Call me back from a land line or something."

Like this kid even knew what that was. And undoubtedly there were no pay phones out in the woods.

"I'm here," the kid replied. And his voice was clearer now.

Luther hadn't lost him. He cursed. "You didn't get her, did you?"

"She was gone," the kid replied.

That had been a concern—that by the time he got some of his crew out there they would have already left. He'd just hoped that Clint was arrogant enough to think he could keep her safe from Luther.

"They're gone?"

"Quarters was still here," the kid said.

Luther's pulse quickened with excitement. "And…"

"He's gotta be dead," the kid confirmed, "with as many times as we hit him and Parker Payne."

It just got better and better. While Rosie might be alive yet, she wouldn't be alive long, not with Clint no longer able to play her hero.

A dead man was nobody's hero.

Chapter 19

The condo was a beautiful town house unit with pale blue walls, white trim and huge windows with views of Lake Michigan. But for some reason, Rosie preferred the small, dark one-room cabin over it. Maybe that was more because of the company than the accommodations.

Logan Payne was not as chatty as his twin. While they looked identical to each other, their personalities were very dissimilar. Logan Payne was very serious and guarded.

Maybe that was how bodyguards were supposed to act. And wasn't he the prototype or something, since he was the one who'd started the Payne Protection Agency?

"You need to step back from the window," he told her, and there was irritation in his deep voice. Probably because it wasn't the first time he'd told her that.

"Shouldn't they be here by now?" she asked. She didn't think the lakeshore hospital would have been that busy in the fall. It wasn't tourist season anymore. "Clint just needed stitches."

She hoped. He'd sworn that bullet had passed through. But what if it was still in there?

Or what if there had been another?

Maybe he'd needed surgery.

Or maybe Parker had fired him for going off on his own. But they'd had no choice, not when the safe house had been compromised. What were they supposed to have done? Stay there and get killed?

She moved back from the window even though she was anxious to keep vigil herself. She was probably more likely to spot some of Luther's crew than Logan Payne would. Sure, he'd once worked for the River City Police Department, but he hadn't worked vice like his twin, like Clint, who'd easily recognized those teenagers at the hospital.

Had Clint spotted more of Luther's crew?

Or had those hunters found the cabin? They'd been acting oddly, like they hadn't wanted her and Clint to walk away. She shivered despite the sunlight pouring through the big window.

"Can you call Parker," she asked, "and find out what's keeping them?"

She knew the fall into the dumpster had broken Clint's phone. He'd had another cell on him later, but she doubted Logan would know the number. But he would definitely have his twin's contact information.

A muscle twitched along Logan's tightly clenched jaw. Maybe he wasn't just irritated with her. Maybe he was worried about his twin, because he pulled out his cell and when he did, his hand shook slightly.

Logan must have had it on speaker because she could hear the ringing, then Parker's voice—which sounded exactly like his twin's—as it went to voice mail.

"Why isn't he picking up?"

"He might have had to shut it off in the hospital," Logan said.

People were supposed to, but as an RN, she knew they rarely did. "But they should be done already. They were leaving right after us."

And it felt as if she'd been at the condo for hours with the reticent Logan. Maybe it only felt like that because she missed Clint, which was crazy.

After Javier had died, she'd never wanted to see Clint Quarters again. But now she couldn't wait to see him.

Logan was worried, too, because he hit Redial again and muttered something like, "Those damn premonitions."

"What?" she asked.

He shook his head. "Just something my mom gets."

Great. So her bodyguard thought his mother was a psychic. Rosie shivered. She really needed Clint, and not just to make sure he was all right but to make sure he was the one to protect her.

She'd been wrong to even consider that another bodyguard might be better for her. Clint really was the only one she could trust.

"Answer your damn phone!" Logan yelled, his control snapping.

And Rosie gasped. Her bodyguard was definitely

rattled, and now his fear was hers. "We need to go to the hospital," she said as she headed toward the stairs that led down to the garage and the SUV.

"No," Logan protested. "We can't leave here. It's not safe."

She didn't care about her safety right now. She cared about Clint. "We need to know where they are and what happened to them."

"I'll find out," Logan said, and he held up his cell. "I'll find them." But before he could call out, a call came in, making his phone vibrate on his palm. He clicked the accept button. "Parker, where the hell are you?"

"Hospital," Parker replied.

"Still?" Logan asked. "You must have been there a while."

"We just got here," Parker said.

"What the hell have you been doing?" Logan demanded to know.

"Getting shot at," his twin replied. "We came under fire before we even got out of the driveway of the cabin." He cursed. "I never saw them." His voice cracked. "But Clint did. If he hadn't knocked me down..." His voice cracked again. "He saved my life."

"That's what he does," Rosie murmured, thinking of all the times Clint had saved hers. Had she thanked him? She couldn't remember if she had or not.

She'd been so stubborn, hanging on to her anger and resentment of him.

"Are you okay?" Logan anxiously asked his twin. "Mom had one of her damn premonitions about you."

"I'm fine," Parker said.

"What about Clint?" Rosie shouted the question so she would be heard.

"Clint…" Parker trailed off.

But Rosie doubted the connection had been lost. She started shaking. There was something in Parker's voice, something like finality. Had Clint given his life for his boss's?

She didn't doubt that he would have—willingly. He'd nearly done that for her time and time again. And she'd never even been nice to him.

Parker was his friend. He wouldn't have hesitated to take a bullet for him. And how many times could the man get hurt during one assignment and still survive?

Her shaking became so violent that her knees nearly folded beneath her. And she couldn't see for the tears blurring her vision.

Clint was gone.

She'd had a feeling, as she'd driven away with Logan Payne, that she might never see Clint again. Not too long ago she'd thought that was what she wanted.

But now all she wanted was Clint.

She needed more than one damn bodyguard, even if that bodyguard was Logan Payne. Clint barely waited until the garage door opened before he jumped out of the SUV and headed up the steps to the main floor of the town house. But he didn't make it far before he was dropped to the floor, his arm pinned behind him.

He grunted in pain.

"Get off him!" a female voice shouted. "Get off him! It's Clint."

"What the hell were you thinking running up here like this?" Logan Payne asked, but he helped him to his feet, which hurt even more than when he'd knocked him down.

Clint grimaced as Parker's twin yanked on his arm, wrenching his wounded shoulder.

"You're hurting him!" Rosie yelled, and she shoved Logan away from him.

The muscular bodyguard stumbled back.

Rosie was fierce. Clint had only seen that fierceness over her brother, though. She'd loved Javier. She couldn't love him. There was too much pain between them, too much blame.

But then she threw her arms around Clint's waist and clung to him. "Are you okay?"

He bobbed his head in a sharp nod. "Yeah, yeah, I'm fine."

"No, you're not," she said, and she drew back to study him through narrowed eyes. "You were shot."

"No, I wasn't."

"Not today, anyway," Parker said as he climbed the stairs. "But I have no idea how you didn't get shot with all the bullets that were flying."

Clint resisted the urge to shudder; he didn't want to scare Rosie or reopen the wound on his shoulder, if Logan hadn't already. "Luther's thugs are used to shooting people point-blank." Like Luther had shot Javier. "They're not trained marksmen."

Fortunately, the trees had taken most of the bullets. And so had the SUV. And when Parker and Clint had returned fire, Luther's crew had fled. They must have been kids again, since they'd moved quickly. They couldn't have been the hunters Clint had happened upon in the woods, and not just because they'd moved so quickly. The ex-cops wouldn't have missed him and Parker like the shooters had. But Clint wouldn't have been surprised if one of the ex-cops had contacted some of Luther's crew with his whereabouts. They'd recognized him.

And the trucks had been gone when he and Parker had finally left for the hospital. Had they been gone before the shooters had arrived? Or had they left when they'd heard the gunfire?

If so, they hadn't been good lawmen.

"Are you all right?" Logan asked his brother, and he studied his face for a long moment.

Parker nodded. "I want to go home and kiss my wife and hug my kids, though."

"Then go," Logan urged him. "You might want to call Mom, too, and let her know you're okay."

Parker shuddered. "So she had one of those damn feelings of hers?"

Logan nodded.

"I wouldn't put it past Luther to put out a hit on me," he said. "And I have no doubt he has one on Clint."

"It's not the first time bodyguards have needed bodyguards," Logan said. "I already called in my team. They're on their way."

"I'm not leaving," Clint said. "Protecting Rosie is my responsibility."

"You can't," Logan said, "when you need to be worried about protecting yourself, too."

But Clint wasn't worried about protecting himself. He was only worried about protecting Rosie. And he didn't trust anyone else to do that.

"I'm not leaving her," he said. And he turned to Parker before his boss could start arguing with him as well. "You can fire me, but I'm still not leaving."

"Clint—"

Parker knew about the promise he'd made her

brother. Clint had told him on the way to the hospital. So he sighed and nodded. "It's okay. You're still on the job."

Logan stared at his brother, as if questioning his judgment. But Clint didn't work for him. And neither did Parker. He didn't say anything, just shook his head and headed to the stairwell.

"I'm keeping a team outside the condo," Parker told Clint. "We've got this."

Clint had been told that before, but he didn't bring that up. He wanted Rosie to believe they were safe.

He only wished that they actually were.

"Go home to your wife and kids," Clint urged his boss.

Parker nodded. "I'm going to do that." But he paused at the top of the stairs to the garage. "Thanks. If you hadn't pushed me down—" he shuddered "—my mom's premonition might have come true."

"It didn't," Clint said. "You're fine."

Parker nodded again and finally headed down the stairs after his brother, leaving Clint alone with Rosie.

And now he was worried about himself. But not about his life—he was worried about his heart.

"How are you really?" she asked.

"Fine," he said. He patted the bandage on his shoulder and tried not to flinch as pain radiated down his arm. "I'm all stitched up and pumped full of antibiotics." That was what had taken so damn long—when all he'd wanted was to be with her, to make sure none of the shooters had seen Logan leave and followed him.

But maybe she'd been safer without him around. Maybe Logan had been right and Clint wasn't the right person to protect her, not if Luther had put out a hit on him, too.

"How are you?" he asked.

She'd changed out of the scrubs she'd been wearing into a loose knit dress that Logan must have stocked in the condo. This place was a lot better equipped than Clint's cabin had been. And hopefully safer.

"I'm fine," she said. But she blinked furiously as if fighting back tears.

He slid his fingers under her chin and tipped it up, so she would meet his gaze. Her eyes glistened with unshed tears. "Oh, Rosie…"

He flinched now. But the pain wasn't in his shoulder. It was in his heart. But it wasn't *his* heart anymore. She had taken it.

He wasn't even sure when it happened. Probably before he'd started protecting her. Probably before Javier had died.

But since Javier had died, Clint knew Rosie didn't want his heart. She didn't want any part of him. But then she rose up on her toes and pressed her mouth to his, kissing him hungrily. So maybe she did want him.

He wanted her. So badly…but he knew that it would be wrong to make love to her again. Last time he had he'd fallen asleep and nearly lost her.

So he summoned all his willpower and stepped back from her. Hurt flashed through her eyes with his rejection.

But he couldn't take the chance that he might lose her again…and this time forever.

"You said your team is all right," Sharon said as she lifted her head from Parker's chest to stare up at him.

He idly stroked her shoulder as she curled against him. His mother had been at his house when he'd arrived home. And after giving him a hug and some time to hug his kids, Grandma had whisked them away.

She'd known—as she always knew things—that he needed to be alone with his wife. He needed to be with Sharon, as close as he could be to her, buried deep inside her. He wouldn't have been surprised if they hadn't just made another baby, their lovemaking had been so intense.

But then, even after years of marriage, it was always intense, always incredible. He loved her so much. He brushed his lips across her forehead. "Yeah, my team is all right."

At least they were for the moment. Clint was all stitched up. The doctor had assured them that the bullet, which must have been small caliber, had passed cleanly through him the night before, hitting nothing vital. The wound from the dumpster was the worse one. But now it was properly stitched, so it would heal.

It wasn't those injuries Parker was worried about, though. He worried about the wounds Clint might still get, and not just physical ones. It was apparent to Parker that Clint had fallen for the witness.

And despite what she'd told Parker a few nights ago, she appeared to have feelings for Clint as well. That was why he'd left them alone together. He'd thought they would take care of each other.

But that might not be the case at all. Maybe they would distract each other so much that Clint wouldn't notice the next time shooters approached.

And as determined as Luther Mills was, Parker had

no doubt that there would be a next time. Rosie wasn't safe, and neither was Clint. Parker had once worried that they might kill each other.

Now he was just worried that they would die together.

Chapter 20

After what had happened between them the previous night in Clint's cabin, Rosie hadn't expected him to reject her. To push her away.

The rejection didn't just sting. It hurt, a pang striking her heart so hard that it took away her breath for a moment. But she was too proud to beg for his touch, for his kiss.

For him.

So she forced herself to shrug it off like it didn't matter. But it did.

He mattered.

She'd been so worried about him. More worried about him than she had been about herself. But she was too proud to admit that, too.

"Have you eaten?" Clint asked.

She hadn't been able to eat because she'd been so worried about him. She shook her head.

"You must be starving then," he said as he moved toward the kitchen.

She wasn't hungry. She wanted him instead, wanted his arms around her, wanted his lips on hers.

After his rejection, she had moved back to the window that Logan had yelled at her for getting too close to. Not that it mattered now. She could see that the other Payne Protection bodyguards had arrived and were standing near their black SUVs. They were ready for another attack.

Was Clint?

Would he reject her if she tried to kiss him again?

Rosie was used to fighting for what she wanted, for having to work for it. Nothing had ever been given to her or to Javier.

So she stepped back from the window and followed him into the kitchen. He moved easily around it, cutting up vegetables that Logan must have brought as he sautéed some thin strips of beef. She hadn't been hungry for food but with the fragrant aroma of it beginning to fill the room, she suddenly was. Her stomach growled.

And Clint smiled at her.

Her breath caught in her lungs. He was so damn good-looking. "I thought you were a bodyguard," she said. "Not a chef."

"I have many talents," he said.

She knew that from the night before. Her body ached to feel his again. She settled onto a barstool at the counter and crossed her legs. "Why aren't you married then?" she asked.

He shrugged. And he didn't wince when he did it. His shoulder must have been feeling better.

She wished she was. But along with the pain of his rejection, she had this nagging jealousy, too. She couldn't believe he was really single. "No live-in girlfriend, either?"

What about the blonde bodyguard?

He snorted. "Landon comes the closest to that. We share a house in the city."

"So he cramps your style," she teased.

He shook his head. "My job does—did. I didn't have time for relationships when I was a vice cop."

"Because you were trying so hard to arrest Luther."

He didn't deny it. But he turned back to his frying pan, tossing in the vegetables he'd cut up. In minutes he put a plate of stir-fry in front of her.

The mention of his preoccupation with Luther reminded her of what it had cost her: her brother. It was good that Clint had pushed her away. They had no future together—because Javier had no future.

"I didn't poison it," he assured her as she hesitated to take a bite.

"Is that why you cooked?" she asked. "You thought I might poison you?"

He nodded. "I thought that…a couple of days ago. Now I'm not so sure you would."

Did he think she cared about him? But, of course, with the way she'd acted when he showed up at the condo, he had every right to think that.

She did care, and she couldn't claim it was just because she was a nurse. Her hand shaking somewhat, she picked up her fork.

And he held up his hands. "Don't stab me with that. I was just teasing."

This was the man her brother had known, the one

he'd idolized. The one who put his life at risk for others—the one who took care of other people. And for the first time she understood why Javier had done what he had. Clint hadn't coerced him; he'd inspired him.

"Are you okay?" he asked.

She nodded. "Just hungry." While the food wasn't what she really wanted, she ate. And it was delicious. Clint knew what he was doing in the kitchen and the bedroom.

"I'll clean up," she offered when he reached for her empty plate. But he helped, standing so close to her at the sink that she could feel the heat from his body. And when she turned her head, she found his close to hers.

He leaned over and brushed his lips across hers.

And her breath caught in her throat. She forced herself to pull back.

And he shook his head. "I'm sorry."

"Why?" she asked. "Are you sorry you kissed me? Are you sorry about last night?"

He shook his head again. "No. I'm sorry I'm not sorry. I'm sorry I want to do it again—when I should be focused only on protecting you."

She gestured toward the window. "There is an army of bodyguards out there. We're safe."

But she didn't feel all that safe, not with this discussion. She was afraid that she was about to beg... her pride be damned.

He nodded. Then he picked her up.

"Clint! Your shoulder—"

But he ignored her protest and headed for the stairs. One flight led down to the garage, another led up to a bedroom. He carried her up. So his shoulders wouldn't have the burden of all her weight, she moved, sliding her legs around his waist.

And he groaned.

"See, I'm too heavy," she said.

"You're too sexy," he said as he reached the top step.

She slid down his body and felt his erection pressing against the fly of his jeans. He wanted her as much as she wanted him.

Maybe more…because he groaned again. "You're killing me."

She wasn't, but Luther was certainly trying. When Clint pulled off his shirt, the fresh bandage reminded her of how much he'd been hurt. Because of her.

And she had hurt him, too, adding to the guilt he'd already felt over her brother's death. She'd blamed him when he'd already been blaming himself.

"I'm sorry," she said.

And he tensed. "Have you changed your mind?"

She had, but not in the way he obviously thought. He stepped back from her and raised his hands like he had in the kitchen. But he wasn't playing now. His eyes were dark and serious.

"I'll sleep on the couch," he said as he leaned over to pick up his shirt.

She caught it in her hands, holding tight to it to pull him toward her. "No," she said. "I want you."

And that was all she needed to say for him to move, to close his arms around her and pull her against his body. He was hard and still tense.

She felt that tension herself, winding tightly inside her. She needed the release she knew he could give her. She needed him. But instead of closing her arms around him, she stepped back.

And his brow furrowed with disappointment...until she reached down and lifted her dress over her head. Then his breath shuddered out in a ragged sigh.

"Rosie." He lifted her again but carried her only the short distance to the bed, with its white metal headboard, before laying her down. Before he joined her, he unbuttoned his jeans and kicked off them and his shoes.

She wanted the boxers gone, too. So she leaned forward and slid them down his lean hips. Her palms glided over his butt, which was as perfect as the rest of him.

He groaned. "You are seriously testing my self-control."

"You have some?" she teased.

And he chuckled. "Apparently not. I know I shouldn't be doing this with you. I'm supposed to be protecting you. Not..."

"What?" she asked.

"Not taking advantage of you."

She laughed now. "You really think that I would let you do that?"

He shook his head. "I didn't think you would ever let me get this close to you," he said. "And I think the only reason you have is because you're in danger. So yeah, I'm taking advantage of you."

She couldn't argue with everything he'd said. They would not have been making love if they hadn't been forced to spend time together. But it was in spending time with him that Rosie had begun to see the man Clint really was, the man her brother had sworn he was.

She shook her head. "Maybe I'm taking advantage

of you," she said. And she trailed her fingers over his washboard abs to the head of his erection.

He gasped. "Rosie…"

And she smiled.

"Maybe you are," he agreed.

"Do you care?"

He shook his head. "You can take advantage of me anytime." But he moved her hand away and gently pushed her back onto the bed. And as he did, he followed her down, pressing his body against hers.

She writhed beneath him. She wore her bra and panties yet. And that was too much. She wanted nothing between them anymore. Not clothes.

Not the past.

She wanted to be as close to him as she could get. Before she could wriggle out of her underwear, he'd unclasped her bra and rolled her panties down her legs. Then he moved his fingers between her legs, stroking her to insanity, as he lowered his mouth and kissed her.

Their lips met, clung, nibbled…their tongues mated. Then he pulled back and slid his mouth down her throat and lower, to her breasts.

He lavished attention on them, stroking his tongue over one nipple, then the other, until she cried out with pleasure. He pulled back and grabbed up his jeans, pulling a condom from the pocket.

She took the packet from him and tore it open. Then she rolled the latex over the length of his erection.

He groaned and murmured, "Rosie…"

She knew he needed a release, too. He was so tense that he was probably about to break in two. Despite the pleasure he'd just given her, she wanted more. She arched her hips, taking him deep as he eased inside her.

They were close—as close as she'd wanted to be to him. She clutched at him, with her legs, with her arms—holding on to him. She never wanted to let him go.

She never wanted the pleasure to end. And he moved, giving her more and more. He held off on his own release until he gave her another orgasm and then another.

She cried out, nearly sobbing his name from the intensity of the pleasure. Then he tensed and joined her, her name a shout on his lips. He slipped out of the bed, disappearing into a bathroom off the bedroom.

He was only steps away from her, but his absence reminded her of how she'd felt when he'd been gone with Parker. He could have been killed. It was a miracle he hadn't been.

He must have had a guardian angel. And she knew who that angel was. Her brother. Thinking of that, she blinked hard, fighting back a rush of tears. She knew what she had to do—for Javier and most especially for Clint.

Clint slid back into bed and rolled Rosie against his side. He wanted to hold her like he had the night before. He wanted to keep her safe, not just until after the trial, but for the rest of their lives.

She probably would have laughed if she knew what he was thinking, that he hoped they could have something permanent. Neither of them had ever known much permanence, growing up the way they had.

People had come and gone in their lives.

Javier was gone.

And because of that, he doubted he could ever have

anything permanent with Rosie. Javier would always be between them. But that was as it should be. Clint was to blame for the kid dying; he didn't deserve to be happy with, of all people, Javier's sister.

He uttered a ragged sigh.

"Are you okay?" she anxiously asked him. "Are you hurting? You probably didn't take a prescription for painkillers, did you?"

"No, I didn't." But not for the reason she thought. He wasn't worried about becoming an addict. He was worried about losing his focus with her. But he'd already done that without the drugs.

She was like a drug to him, though.

He could easily become addicted to her, to making love with her. To being with her.

"I'm fine," he said.

"For now," she said. "But Luther will try again. He'll find us."

Clint pulled her closer and stroked his fingers down her back. "I will protect you," he promised.

"Or die trying…"

"Rosie—"

"I want to see Luther," she said.

He tensed. "What?"

He must have fallen asleep. He must have been dreaming. She couldn't really want to visit the man who had murdered her brother right in front of her.

But then she'd just slept with the man she blamed for her brother's death: him.

He shook his head. "No. That's crazy."

He wasn't even sure it would be allowed. The eyewitness visiting the murder suspect?

"I have to," she insisted.

"He's trying to kill you," he reminded her.

"He can't do that in jail," she said. "I will be on one side of the glass, he'll be on the other. I'll be safer there than anywhere else."

Clint doubted that. He doubted she would be safe anywhere while Luther Mills was alive. Even after the trial, he probably wouldn't give up. He would want her dead out of vengeance for sending him away.

"Rosie, it's a bad idea," he said. And he was understating it.

"I know Luther," she said. "Maybe I can get through to him."

"How?" How could she get through to a man who had no conscience? No soul?

But she persisted. "Maybe I can get him to accept the responsibility for Javier's death."

He snorted. Luther Mills wasn't him. He wasn't going to take responsibility for any of the horrible things he'd done. And if Rosie truly knew him, she knew that. So what was she really up to?

"I want to try to talk him into taking a plea deal," she said.

If she could, then it would all be over.

But he doubted Luther would ever back down.

"That's the prosecutor's job, not yours," he said. And he doubted ADA Jocelyn Gerber would be very damn happy if Rosie visited the defendant.

But that wasn't going to happen.

Clint would rather die than let Rosie get anywhere near the man determined to kill her.

Luther had had a lot of visitors during his stay in jail. But he'd never expected this person to visit him.

He wasn't even sure it was allowed. He picked up the phone on the other side of the glass and gestured for her to do the same. Once she held it to her ear, he asked, "Does ADA Gerber know you're here?" he asked.

Rosie shook her head.

"Does Clint Quarters know?" he asked. Or was the man dead like his crew had claimed? He hadn't seen anything on the news to indicate they'd told him the truth, though. But maybe it had been kept quiet.

Chief Woodrow Lynch was somehow related to the Payne Protection Agency. He might have ordered the deaths kept out of the media. But then the chief was new to River City. He didn't have the resources that Luther did.

He should have heard something by now if Clint and Parker Payne were really dead.

"Clint brought me here," Rosie said.

And Luther cursed. Apparently that damn bodyguard hadn't used up all nine of his lives yet. But Luther wouldn't rest until he'd taken every last one of them.

"You thought he was dead," she surmised.

Rosie had always been smart. The smartest girl in class when they'd gone to school together. Not that Luther had gone to school for very long.

He'd found easier ways to make money. But Rosie had never been impressed with that—with him—like he'd wanted to impress her.

"Stop," she told him. "Stop trying to hurt Clint."

He narrowed his eyes and studied her. Was she trying to trap him? Trying to get him to say something incriminating? Was that the reason she was here?

Now he didn't feel so damn bad about having to kill

her. He even wished he could have the satisfaction of doing it himself—of doing it here. But he couldn't get through that glass to wrap his hands around her neck like he wanted. To squeeze the life from her beautiful body.

"I would have thought you'd want Clint Quarters hurt," Luther said. "That you'd want him dead for what he did to Javier."

"You killed Javier," she said with a dead-calm certainty that would have every juror voting guilty. If she made it to the witness stand...

She could *not* make it to the witness stand.

"But it was Quarters that made Javi a rat," he said. "And you know rats always get exterminated."

She flinched and blinked hard, but she didn't cry. Rosie was tough. That was another thing he'd always admired about her. Until now.

Now he wished she were scared, scared enough to take back her testimony.

"Clint Quarters isn't a rat," she said.

"Every cop is." Even the ones who helped him out. Maybe especially them.

"He's not a cop anymore," she said.

"Once a cop, always a cop," Luther said.

She shook her head. "Leave him alone. Stop trying to kill him."

So she was here about Quarters, not about herself? Luther felt a punch to the gut as jealousy twisted his stomach into knots. Had she actually fallen for a cop?

Or had she fallen for the bodyguard who kept saving her life? That was Luther's fault; he'd given Clint the chance to play her hero. He had to end this now. "You know what it'll take for that happen."

She shivered. "You don't want me to testify."

"You're a smart girl, Rosie. I don't have to spell it out for you." And he damn well wasn't going to when she might have been recording him.

"I won't," she agreed.

Too easily.

He knew how much she had loved her brother. There was no way she would let his killer go free. And now she didn't see that his killer was Quarters. She saw that his killer was Luther.

He chuckled. "Yeah, right…"

"No, I swear I won't," she said. "If you stop trying to kill Clint, I'll go to Ms. Gerber and tell her I won't testify against you."

He snorted at her blatant lie. How stupid did she think he was?

"You have someone in her office," she said. "You'll know that I'm telling the truth. I'll go right to her and tell her I refuse to testify."

He would know right away. But now he knew something else. As much as Rosie had loved her brother, she loved Clint Quarters more. And now, with jealousy twisting his stomach into knots, Luther was even more determined to kill the man.

But the deal she was offering…

He could get out sooner once he got rid of that other evidence. He sighed. "He's not going to appreciate your gesture, Rosie," he warned her. "All Clint Quarters has ever wanted is me behind bars."

She flinched now, so he knew she knew about that stupid cousin of Clint's. The boy had been skimming product. So Luther had forced him to shoot up all of it he'd stolen. He'd needed to set an example, especially back then when his operation was just really starting to take off.

"That's all he'll ever care about, Rosie," Luther warned her. "He doesn't care about you. He only cares about making sure you make it to that witness stand. If you refuse to testify, you'll be of no use to him anymore. He'll want nothing to do with you."

Her face flushed, but she denied her intentions regarding her bodyguard. "All I want is for you to stop trying to have him killed."

"And you know what I want," he told her.

But even if she went to the assistant DA like she was promising, Luther had no intention of holding up his end of the bargain. He wanted Clint Quarters dead even more now than he had before.

He wanted him dead more now because Clint had the one thing Luther had never been able to get, despite all his money and power: Rosie Mendez.

But Quarters wouldn't have her for very damn long.

Once Luther had her bodyguard killed, his crew would have no problem getting to Rosie. And she would learn just what her sacrifice for Quarters cost her—not just justice for her brother but her own damn life as well.

Chapter 21

Rosie was more fearful about this meeting than she'd been about the one with Luther Mills. She knew Luther. She knew what to expect.

She didn't know Jocelyn Gerber. Maybe the woman would be secretly thrilled because she actually was one of Luther's crew. Or maybe she would be furious because she was all about winning—as Rosie had suspected earlier.

Clint had gone along for this meeting with the same begrudging agreement as he had the last. He hadn't been able to go with her inside the visiting room to talk to Luther, though. And she'd been happy about that.

She didn't want him to sit in on this meeting, either. "Please," she implored him. "Can you give us a minute alone?"

Clint shook his head. He clearly didn't trust Jocelyn Gerber any more than she did. "That's not possible."

"I'm not leaving, either," Landon Myers told her.

And Jocelyn grimaced. "Bodyguards don't understand that sometimes we need to be alone." The assistant district attorney sounded like she *really* needed to be alone.

So she could talk to Luther?

Or had she already?

Rosie shivered as she noticed the coldness in the woman's icy blue eyes. And she knew that she already knew...

"What the hell were you thinking?" Jocelyn asked. But she directed the question at Clint instead of her. "Why would you take her to the jail?"

She didn't wait for his response before she turned on Rosie. "And what the hell were *you* thinking? You might have jeopardized the whole case!"

"What?" Landon asked. Clearly, he didn't know what had happened.

So Jocelyn informed him. "She went to see Luther Mills." She pointed a shaking finger at Clint. "And he took her!"

Landon turned to Clint, his brow furrowed with confusion. "What was the deal? Did you have her wear a wire?"

"Like Luther Mills would have said anything incriminating!" Jocelyn exclaimed. But then she turned back to Rosie and asked, "Did he?"

She shook her head. Luther had been careful. But he'd gotten his point across. She knew what she had to do for Clint.

Jocelyn shook her head, and her curtain of black hair swung back and forth across her shoulders. "His lawyer could have a field day with this—with you—when he cross-examines you on the witness stand."

"He won't," Rosie told her.

"The man is a shark," Jocelyn said. "Of course he will. He's going to tear you apart."

And Clint tensed, his hands curling into fists, as if he'd taken the ADA literally.

"No, he won't," Rosie said, "because I have no intention of testifying."

"What!" Clint beat Jocelyn to the exclamation.

And the ADA turned on him again. "That's why you shouldn't have taken her there. He intimidated her into changing her mind."

"You don't think all the attempts on her life were intimidation enough?" Landon asked.

Clint stared at Rosie. "I promised I would keep you safe."

He had. But she knew what that could and probably would cost him: his life.

And that wasn't a sacrifice she was willing to let him make. Not for her and not so he could keep his promise to her dead brother. Javier wouldn't have wanted that, either. He'd cared too much about Clint.

"Now there's no need," she said. "I'm safe now." And more importantly, so was he.

Clint snorted. "You really believe that Luther Mills will keep his word to you? That he won't have you killed the minute you walk out of here with no protection?"

She shivered. Would Luther keep his word? Surely he knew that if he sent any more of his crew after her and Clint, their deal was off. She would gladly testify then.

"Quarters is right," Jocelyn said. "There is no way that Luther Mills will let you stay alive—not when you are the greatest threat to his freedom. You have to testify."

"You should be glad that I changed my mind," Rosie told her.

And the woman's smooth brow furrowed. "Why the hell would I be happy?"

"Because now you're safe, too," she said. "He won't have any reason to threaten you or the others if there's not enough evidence to bring him to trial."

Jocelyn gasped, as if horrified. "There's still enough evidence." She glanced at Landon. "The CSI tech—Wendy."

"Wendy Thompson," Landon said. "Hart Fisher is protecting her."

"She hasn't changed her mind about testifying, has she?" Ms. Gerber anxiously asked.

Landon shrugged.

"We need to talk to her," Jocelyn said, and it was clear she was scrambling now to save her case. She was definitely not on Luther's payroll like Rosie had wondered from time to time. "We need to make sure Mills hasn't gotten to her like he has this witness."

Jocelyn turned back to Rosie, and her lips were pursed in disgust. "What did he give you?" she asked. "Money? What did it take for you to sell out? To sell the justice your brother deserves?"

Rosie flinched with regret. "You don't know my brother," she told the other woman. "Don't act like you know what he deserves or wanted."

He wanted her and Clint to be together. That was the dying wish Javier had expressed to her. She didn't expect that to happen now. Clint couldn't even look at her. But she knew that Javier wouldn't want his idol or her to die for that justice for him.

The woman turned on one pointy heel and headed toward the stairs leading down to the garage. Landon hurried after her, but he had one comment for Clint before he headed down the stairwell. "What the hell?"

Clint shook his head. But the minute they were alone, he repeated his friend's question. "What the hell?"

Clint could barely contain his fury. He had never been so angry with Rosie—not even when she'd tossed him out of her brother's funeral. That, he'd understood. She'd blamed him for Javier's death.

And she was right. He blamed himself, too.

But this…

His stomach pitched, churning with anger and regret. "I knew I shouldn't have taken you to the jail."

But he'd given in because she'd been so determined that he'd figured she would have sneaked away from him had he refused to take her. And he hadn't wanted her to go alone.

He hadn't wanted her out on own. He hadn't wanted her in danger. But he'd put her in even more than he'd realized when he'd sneaked past the guards at the lakeshore condo and taken her to the jail in River City.

"What did he say to you?" Clint asked. If only he could have gone into the visitation room with her…

Then he would know.

What threat had Luther made that had her this scared? Scared enough to let the drug dealer get away with murdering her brother?

"He didn't threaten me," Rosie said.

And Clint snorted his disbelief. "Of course he didn't. He didn't have to. He's been threatening you for days every time he sent his crew after you."

She shivered.

"I can't believe this," he said. And he shook his head in disbelief. "You were so angry about your brother's death. What happened to that anger? To that determination to get justice for Javier?"

"Javier wouldn't want me to get killed," she said.

And he couldn't argue with that. Javier had wanted to keep his sister safe. But he'd given that responsibility to Clint. "No, he wouldn't," he agreed. "That's why he made me promise to protect you."

She nodded. "I know that's why you've been so determined to be my bodyguard, because you already feel so guilty about not keeping him safe."

That had been his reason in the beginning. But then he'd fallen for her. Hell, he'd fallen for her even before he'd made that promise to Javier.

But now he wasn't even sure he knew who she was. The woman with whom he'd fallen in love would have never let her brother's killer go free. Now he didn't know how he felt about her. So he just shrugged in response to her statement.

Then he added, "And it is my job. I'm a bodyguard."

"It's hypocritical of you to say I'm giving up on justice for Javier," she said. "You did that when you quit the River City PD."

"I quit because I thought you were going to follow through," he said, "that you, of all people, would make sure Javier got justice."

She snorted disparagingly at him. "You thought I

was going to get Luther for you…" She shook her head. "He's your white whale. Not mine."

His stomach churned again, but he wasn't upset about Luther. "What about Javier?"

Her brother had loved her so much. All he'd wanted was her respect again, to make it up to her for everything she'd done for him his entire life.

A life that Luther Mills had cut too short.

"He's dead," she said. "And Luther's going to prison will not bring him back. Nothing will." She walked away from Clint then and climbed the stairs to the loft as if she had the weight of the world on her shoulders.

And maybe she did. Or she had. But refusing to testify should have taken off that weight, if she had been afraid for her life. If she truly believed not testifying was the right thing…

She didn't.

She couldn't.

Why the hell had she changed her mind? He was tempted to go meet with Luther himself—to find out what threat Luther had used that had scared her so much that she wasn't even the woman Clint had thought she was.

But maybe he and her brother had been wrong about her all along.

Maybe she wasn't the strong, determined woman he and Javier had thought she was. Maybe Rosie was just like most everyone else who lived in the area of River City that Luther had claimed as his: maybe she was one of his crew.

Woodrow met Parker at the door to his office and clasped his shoulders before pulling him into a quick hug. When he stepped back, Parker stared at him in surprise. Woodrow wasn't usually a demonstrative person, so he must have shocked his stepson.

"Your mother's wearing off on me," he told Parker. Penny was innately affectionate.

The younger man smiled with love for his mother. "She has that effect on people."

"She had me worried," Woodrow admitted. Those damn premonitions of hers. "I was thinking I might have been wrong to hire you."

Parker groaned. "So you heard about the witness…"

That wasn't what he'd been referring to, but a weary sigh slipped through his lips. And he nodded.

"Jocelyn Gerber called you," Parker guessed. Correctly.

Woodrow nodded again and added, "Ms. Gerber is quite upset." Which was an understatement.

"She's blaming the Payne Protection Agency," Parker said.

"She blamed me," Woodrow said.

Parker's mouth slid into a lopsided grin. "For hiring us."

That had been the gist of it. But it was also because he had a leak in his department. She was determined to overlook the one that had to be in hers, though.

Of course, it wasn't really her department. She wasn't the district attorney, even though she'd been acting like it since Amber Kozminski was out on her maternity leave. She and her husband, Logan Payne's brother-in-law and bodyguard, Milek Kozminski, had just had their second child, a baby girl.

"I'm sorry for letting you down," Parker said, and he looked like a son who'd disappointed his father.

But none of the Paynes was a disappointment.

"You and your team have kept the principals alive." Woodrow was learning protection language since marrying into a family of bodyguards. "And since Ms. Mendez is alive, there is always a chance she will change her mind about testifying."

Parker released a ragged sigh. "True. But she has to stay alive, and I'm not sure she'll agree to stay in protection since she's not testifying."

The younger man looked upset, and it probably wasn't about the attempt on his life that he had narrowly escaped. Parker had survived many, many more attempts than that.

"What is it?" Woodrow asked.

Parker shook his head. "I'm wondering if I made a big mistake."

"How's that?"

"When I matched up bodyguard to principal..." Parker pushed one of his hands through his thick black hair. "Clint warned me that she wouldn't want him."

"And she told the two of us the same thing," Woodrow remembered.

"I just didn't think she'd go to this extreme to get rid of him," Parker said with another ragged sigh.

"It seemed as though you'd changed her mind... with what you said about her brother."

"I thought she had changed her mind about Clint," Parker said. He snorted with self-derision. "I actually thought she was starting to care about him. But he was probably right—she'll never be able to forgive him for her brother becoming an informant."

"I'm not so sure," Woodrow said. When ADA Gerber had called him, he'd had a thought about Ms.

Mendez's reason for backing out of testifying against Luther Mills. Maybe it was because she *had* forgiven Clint. "Quarters is the one who's gotten hurt protecting her."

And Ms. Mendez didn't seem like the type of person who cared just about herself. If she had been the only one in danger, he doubted she would have changed her mind about testifying against her brother's killer.

Parker's blue eyes narrowed as he considered what Woodrow had said.

"Ms. Gerber is having the recording of their visit sent to her office," Woodrow also informed him. So they would know soon enough what had motivated Rosie Mendez's change of heart. And maybe that was exactly what it was.

A change of heart regarding her bodyguard.

Parker snorted again. "Does Jocelyn Gerber actually believe Luther might have said something incriminating?"

"I think she's more interested in what Ms. Mendez had to say, in finding out the reason for her visit." But Woodrow, who was still a newlywed, had a feeling he already knew what that reason was.

Or rather who: Clint Quarters.

Chapter 22

Luther was right. All Clint cared about was putting him behind bars for the rest of his life. He didn't care about her. He'd only been protecting her because she was the witness, because she was the one who could finally give him what he wanted, what he'd sacrificed so much to get: a personal life, even her brother...

Her testimony would have gotten the conviction against Luther Mills that Clint had wanted since his cousin had died. Maybe Jocelyn Gerber could get that conviction without Rosie's testimony.

She hoped like hell that was truly the case. Or she would have sacrificed justice for her brother for the safety of a man who didn't even care about her.

Tears stung her eyes, but she blinked them back. Rosie was not one who gave in to tears. All crying accomplished was puffy eyes and a red nose. She didn't need either of those.

And she didn't need Clint Quarters. Thanks to her meeting with Luther, she didn't need him to protect her anymore. And she certainly didn't need him to love her.

Rosie had gotten along just fine without Clint Quarters. Hell, she'd been better. He'd brought nothing but pain to her life.

She glanced at the bed in the loft area of the condo and begrudgingly had to admit that he hadn't brought her just pain. He'd also brought her more pleasure than she'd ever experienced before.

But that was just sex, which had probably been heightened in intensity because of all the danger they'd been in. Since she'd never felt anything like that before, she must have confused it with love.

But she couldn't actually love Clint Quarters—not after she'd spent so much time hating him.

Their feelings seemed to have reversed now. He'd looked like he'd hated her—or at least been totally disgusted with her—when she'd refused to testify. He didn't understand that she'd done it for him.

And she didn't want him to know. She felt like a fool for falling for him. Is that what happened to bodyguards? Did the person they were protecting fall for them? Rosie must have just mistaken gratitude for love.

She would not make that mistake again. She would not have any reason to be grateful to Clint anymore.

She didn't need his protection. What she needed was to get away from him. Far away.

So that she didn't ache for him anymore. So that she didn't want him… He hadn't come upstairs with her. As disgusted as he'd been with her, he clearly did not want her anymore. And that was good.

She didn't want him, either. Tears stung her eyes again, but she fought them back. She was not going to cry.

No. She was going to get the hell out of there. But how?

Not only was Clint inside but there were also body-guards outside. They were looking for people trying to get in, though—not out. She and Clint had managed to slip past them easily enough when they'd gone to the jail earlier.

She could manage to do that again. Without Clint. She would have to manage without him now.

She heard the deep rumble of his voice. He must have been on his cell phone because she hadn't heard anyone else come into the condo.

She crept down the stairs from the loft bedroom. There was just a small landing between those steps and the ones leading down to the garage. If she could cross over that landing without Clint noticing her...

She had a chance of escaping him.

As she descended the last step, she saw him. He didn't see her, though. His back was to her as he stood at the window, looking down on the street below. The cell phone was pressed to his ear.

She tensed, worried that he might see her reflection in the glass. The sun was shining brightly as it began to descend over Lake Michigan. It was a beautiful sunset. One she wished she could have shared with him.

But she couldn't share anything with him now. She needed to get away from him before she cast aside her pride and begged for him to understand. She hurried over the landing before he turned—before he saw her.

She crept down that last flight, flinching at the soft

creak of each step beneath her weight. Finally she reached the last one, the step onto the cement floor of the garage. There was a service door at the back of it. She wasn't certain where it opened—onto an alley or a yard.

Even if she was out of his presence, could she escape him? She'd thought of him so often since Javier's death, but she'd been angry then.

She wasn't angry anymore.

She was just…

Devastated. Devastated that Luther was right. All Clint wanted was him behind bars—whatever the cost. Javier's life. Hers…

His. He obviously didn't care.

She cared. No matter how much she wished she didn't. She cared. At least Clint would be safe. She carefully pushed open the service door onto an alley. Someone stood at one end of it, his hand near his holster.

She turned the other way. If there was a guard there, she didn't see him or her. So sticking close to the shadows of the buildings lining both sides of the alley, she hurried out onto the street.

She had her purse and enough money in her savings to get far away from River City. But before she went anywhere, there was someone she needed to tell goodbye.

"It doesn't make sense," Clint told Landon. And that was what bothered him most. Sure, he'd considered, for a few moments when fury had gripped him, that she could be part of Luther's crew. But he knew better.

Javier had become an informant for Clint because

he'd felt so bad about selling drugs for the guy after all the years his sister had fought to keep him away from Luther. She wouldn't have done that if she'd been part of the crew herself.

No. Rosie had fought hard to have a better life for herself and her younger brother. So why the hell would she stop fighting now?

"So tell me what Luther said to her," Clint implored. Landon had to have been present when Jocelyn Gerber played the recorded conversation.

Landon's ragged sigh rattled the cell phone. "Somebody at the jail must have messed with the tape. It had been wiped clean."

Clint cursed. Was there no one Luther couldn't get to? Clint would have thought that person was Rosie—until now—until she'd backed out of testifying.

"I know he has a cell phone," Clint said. He'd called Luther from that kid's phone. "A guard must have smuggled that to him."

"Jocelyn's asking a judge to subpoena the bank records of every corrections officer at the jail." Landon sounded impressed, which surprised the hell out of Clint. Usually he sounded disgusted by the ambitious but ineffectual assistant district attorney.

"Even if she can prove Luther bribed them, that's petty stuff," Clint said. "He needs to get convicted of Javier's murder." Or the poor kid would have died for nothing.

How could his sister, the person who had sworn she loved him most, allow that to happen?

He shook his head, unable to believe that she would not testify against his killer.

"Talk to her," Landon urged him.

"I tried."

"Did you talk or yell?" his friend asked. From living with Clint, he knew him well. Clint didn't often get angry, but when he did, he wasn't always as diplomatic as he should be. He certainly hadn't been diplomatic with Rosie.

"Oh, hell," he murmured.

And Landon chuckled. "Yeah, try again. And do it nicely this time."

"I've tried to be nice to Rosie Mendez before," Clint reminded him. "It doesn't have any effect on her."

"You getting hurt certainly did," Landon said. "She was concerned about you."

"That's because she's a nurse," Clint said. "It's just part of who she is."

Landon snorted. "Yeah, right. And the reason you've been so willing to risk your life for hers is just because you're a bodyguard. C'mon, Clint, you're not fooling anyone."

Least of all his best friend. But apparently, he had fooled Rosie. She thought all he cared about was busting Luther Mills. She didn't know that he cared about her, too.

Too much.

Clint sighed now and murmured, "Damn you."

Landon chuckled as he disconnected their call. He knew he'd made his point.

Clint pocketed his cell and moved toward the stairwell. He climbed the steps to the loft. But when he reached the top floor, he didn't see her. She wasn't lying on the bed. She must have not even sat on it because it was neatly made. She wasn't on the chaise, either. And the bathroom door stood open, nobody inside.

"Rosie!" he called out.

How had she slipped past him?

He hurried down the stairs, missing a few steps in his haste. She wasn't on the main level. He would have seen her. So he continued down to the garage. The SUV was parked inside yet. If she'd opened the overhead door, he would have heard the motor of the opener. He wished she'd tried to take it. But obviously she'd slipped out the service door; it wasn't closed completely. He pushed it open and hurried out into the alley. But he didn't get far before he heard a gun cock.

He froze.

It could have been one of the other bodyguards. Or it could have been one of Luther's crew cocking that weapon. And if Luther's crew had found the condo, then Rosie had run right out to them.

And that was Clint's fault. If he'd reacted better to her decision not to testify...

Maybe if he had been more understanding and less judgmental...

Maybe she wouldn't have run away from him. Unless that had been her reason for refusing to testify—so she wouldn't have to have a bodyguard anymore.

But even though she'd told Luther she wouldn't testify, Clint doubted the killer had taken back the hit he'd put out on her.

Luther Mills would still want her dead, so that there was no chance that Rosie could ever change her mind about testifying against him.

But now, with a gun in his back, Clint couldn't protect her. He couldn't even protect himself.

* * *

Luther reached for the cell vibrating in the pocket of his jail jumpsuit. Damn, he couldn't wait until he got back in his own clothes. And that had to be happening soon.

He'd told his lawyer that the prosecution was about to lose their star witness. His lawyer had gotten nervous, hadn't wanted anything to do with murder. Coward.

Luther had assured him his hands would stay clean. As clean as they were when the sleazeball only represented the richest clients. And as Luther knew, it wasn't easy to get rich within the law.

He'd had to break it.

Just like he'd had to break his promise to Rosie. He hadn't removed the hit on Clint. Or on her.

"Yeah," he answered his phone.

"We found the latest safe house."

He grinned. It helped having a source with knowledge of the Payne Protection Agency. "That's good."

"Even better...she slipped out by herself."

Clint Quarters let her out of his sight? He had probably been furious when she'd said she wasn't going to testify. Even as hot as Rosie was, she would never be as important to Clint as getting a conviction against him. By now she had to know she'd fallen for the wrong man.

That must have been why she'd slipped away from him.

Luther chuckled. "Did you take care of her?"

"I wasn't sure what you wanted us to do now," the caller replied.

Luther heard the reluctance in the man's voice, and

he didn't like it. Obviously, he'd hired another coward. And Luther didn't suffer cowards any more than he did traitors.

"I paid you to do a job," he said. "You're not getting any more money until that job is done."

"I followed her," the caller admitted.

"Then finish her," Luther said.

Rosie Mendez had to die, not just so that she couldn't testify against him. She had to die because she'd done the unforgivable: she'd fallen in love with Clint Quarters.

Chapter 23

She always had so much trouble finding his marker. The stone was so small that it didn't stick up above the grass. But she'd walked to his grave so many times that she should have known where it was even without the marker.

She wished she could have afforded a better monument. She wished that she could have done more to honor her baby brother.

"You deserved so much more," she murmured, and tears stung her eyes. She furiously blinked them back to focus on that marker, which recorded Javier's date of birth and date of death.

He had deserved more than the twenty years he'd lived. As his older sister, she'd been the one who had always taken care of him. Their drug-addicted mother certainly hadn't been capable. So Rosie, eight years his senior, had raised him and protected him.

And loved him.

She couldn't fight the tears anymore. They spilled over and ran down her face, dripping onto the ground—onto Javier's grave.

Clint was right. Javier deserved justice. Her going to Luther, even for Clint, had been an act of betrayal against both men. Neither of them wanted Luther to get away with his crimes.

That was why Javier had become Clint's informant. If he hadn't felt like it was the right thing to do, he wouldn't have done it—no matter how much pressure Clint might have put on him. She'd thought it was a lot, but now she had to admit the truth she'd been avoiding.

She never should have blamed Clint for Javier's death. She'd only added to the guilt he'd already put on himself, a guilt he shouldn't be carrying.

Would Luther's conviction help relieve that guilt? Was that why it was so important to him—not just because of his cousin but because of Javier, too?

She could understand that. She could also understand his being upset with her. She was upset with herself at that moment. She'd made a terrible mistake. She needed to tell Clint. She needed to tell the assistant district attorney, too. But when she turned away from Javier's marker, she slammed into the body of the man who'd walked up behind her.

She hadn't heard him approach. But then she'd been crying, so she'd heard only the sound of her broken sobs. She lifted trembling hands to her face and brushed away her tears. Then she blinked and focused on him.

If he hadn't been wearing his navy blue River City PD uniform, Rosie might not have recognized him.

Even then it took her a moment to place him—so much had happened in the past few days.

"Officer Maynard," she greeted him. "I'm so glad to see that you're doing well." He'd been hurt that night at her apartment, the night Clint had been hurt. But he looked better than Clint.

She could see no visible signs of the injury he had sustained. A concussion? Was that what the chief had said he had?

"Ms. Mendez," he greeted her back.

"Did Ms. Gerber send you to find me?" she asked. "Or the chief?" But how would either of them have known where to find her?

Clint was the only one who might have figured it out—because only Clint knew how much she had loved her brother. No wonder he'd been so shocked that she had decided not to testify.

Officer Maynard shook his head. "No. They didn't send me." And he drew his gun from his belt and pointed it at her. "Luther Mills sent me."

She didn't have to ask him why. She knew that he was going to kill her. And just like Clint had warned her, she'd been a fool to trust Luther Mills. If he still intended to kill her, he certainly still intended to kill Clint as well.

Clint had known exactly where to find Rosie. Apparently, he wasn't the only one. The officer must have followed Rosie from the condo since he'd beaten Clint to her. His heart beat fast and hard as he saw the gun the officer pointed at her. But when Clint stepped out from behind a monument, he acted as though he hadn't seen it.

"Good work, Officer," he praised the young man.

"You found her quickly. From those weeks of protecting her, you must have figured out where she would be."

Rosie shook her head, her brown eyes wild with fear, and the officer whirled toward Clint, his gun pointing at him. Clint preferred that to having the weapon on Rosie. He kept his hands open, so the officer could see he had no weapon on him.

It was in the waistband of his jeans, at the small of his back. He'd given up the holster since it had irritated his shoulder wound. But hopefully, since he wasn't wearing it, the officer would think he was unarmed. Clint hoped he could draw his gun fast enough to save her.

"I can take it from here, Officer," Clint continued. "And there are more Payne Protection bodyguards in the parking lot, so she will have plenty of security. You don't have to worry about her."

Like he was worried...

So damn worried.

Especially when she shouted, "No, Clint! He's working for Luther."

The cop whirled back toward Rosie, and Clint drew his weapon. He knew it was too late now for the guy to just walk away and pretend that it had all been a misunderstanding. But before Clint could pull the trigger, the man jumped behind Rosie, using her as a human shield. And he pressed his gun against her temple.

"No," Clint said. "You don't want to do this."

The young officer's eyes were wild with a desperation that made him capable of anything.

"If you'd wanted to kill her, you could have anytime when you were protecting her," Clint pointed out.

The officer shook his head. "Not if I wanted to get

away with it. I told Luther that. But he wouldn't listen. He just kept pushing. He doesn't care about anyone but himself."

"No, he doesn't," Rosie vehemently agreed. "So why would you trust him?"

"Why would you?" Clint asked her. "You had to know that he wasn't going to take the chance you might change your mind about testifying. He was going to kill you anyway."

The officer glanced from Rosie to him, following their argument. She opened her mouth to say something else, but the young man shook her as if she were a doll. "Shut up!" he yelled. "Shut up!"

"The other bodyguards will hear you," Clint warned him. But he was bluffing. He'd come alone to the cemetery. He'd wanted to talk to Rosie without an audience. He hadn't realized that someone might have beaten him to her.

But he should have known—Luther always seemed to be one step ahead of them. Now he understood why. He'd had someone on his crew who'd worked Rosie's protection duty. But yet the officer shouldn't have known where the safe house was.

Who else was working for Luther?

The officer glanced around and then narrowed his eyes with suspicion.

Clint should have known better than to bluff. Landon always joked about how bad he was at it.

"You can't kill us both," Clint pointed out to him. "You might be able to get a round in her before I kill you. But make no mistake, you will die."

The young officer's eyes grew even wilder with desperation.

Clint cocked his gun. "And I'm not going to wait for you to fire the first shot." Because that would have been the smart thing—for the kid to have already taken his shot, to have fired at Clint first.

But he was such a rookie, he might not have even had to draw his weapon on a suspect before, let alone an innocent person like Rosie.

"Don't kill him," Rosie whispered.

The guy didn't yell at her to shut up this time.

"You'll need him to testify against Luther." Then she squeezed her eyes shut, as if expecting him to pull the trigger that second.

But the young officer laughed. "You better just kill me," he told Clint, "because there's no way in hell I would ever be stupid enough to testify against Luther Mills."

His comment jarred Clint. How had he expected Rosie to do something no one else—but her dead brother—had been brave enough to do? That bravery had already cost Javier his life. Maybe she had been stupid to even think about testifying. And Clint had been even stupider to expect her to do it.

"Just put down the gun," Clint implored him. He didn't want to kill anyone, but most of all not a cop. This man had once been like him, had once cared about law and order. Clint wasn't certain where it had all gone wrong or how Luther had gotten to him. "Nobody has to die."

The young man shook his head. "Luther ordered it." He expelled a shaky sigh. "Pretty much everybody who's touched the case against him is going to die."

A chill chased down Clint's spine. The chief had been right to bring in bodyguards. The Payne Protection Agency was the only chance of this trial actually taking place. But he—Clint—was Rosie's only chance of survival.

Somehow, he had to get the officer to take that gun away from her head—because even if Clint took the shot, the guy could reflexively pull the trigger and kill her even as he was dropping to the ground.

"You're not going to get away with this," Clint warned him. "You're never going to collect whatever Luther is paying you."

The guy flinched. So this was about money for him. But just in case…

Clint asked, "Or is he threatening you or someone you care about?"

The officer glanced away from Clint, as if unable to meet his gaze.

"It is all about money," Clint said heavily, disappointed. So the cop had turned for greed, no other reason. "Money you're never going to collect. So killing her is pointless."

The guy snorted. "Killing her is the whole point, man. She's the witness! She has to die!"

And Clint knew he had no choice. Someone was going to die. Here and now. He only hoped that it wasn't Rosie. Not only would he be breaking his promise to Javier, and right on the man's grave, but he would also be losing the woman he loved.

He should have told her. Now he might never have the chance.

Parker no longer had any qualms about being called to Chief Lynch's office. Woodrow wasn't the principal. After that hug he had given Parker earlier today, they weren't just working together. They were family. He'd already known that, of course. But until that hug, until he'd realized how much his mother's husband cared about him, Parker hadn't felt it. Now Woodrow wasn't just his stepfather; he was his dad.

That didn't make what he had to tell the man any easier, so he hesitated for just a moment before knocking on the office door of Chief Woodrow Lynch.

"Come in," Woodrow called out.

Parker opened it up and stepped inside, and as he did, he uttered an apology immediately. "I'm sorry. We lost the witness."

Woodrow tensed. "She's dead?"

"She sneaked out of the safe house," he explained. "She has no protection, so it's only a matter of time before one of Luther's crew gets to her."

"What happened to Quarters?"

Parker had thought the only way Rosie would get away from him was if he was dead. "He's out looking for her."

"He'll know where to look," the chief assured him, more like a father would rather than a client or a boss. "He'll find her."

"I'm sure he will." But would it be too late? Not just for Rosie but for Clint, too?

Parker glanced down at the cell phone in his hand, willing it to ring, willing Clint to call him. "He refused to take anyone along with him," he admitted. And even though other bodyguards had tried to follow him, he'd lost them. "He has no backup."

Woodrow cursed. "Damn fool."

Parker hoped Clint was just a damn fool and not a

dead one. He shook his head. "Maybe he thought he could talk her back into testifying if he went alone."

But a dead woman couldn't testify.

"This is a mess," the chief said with a ragged sigh.

And Parker figured he wasn't talking about just Clint and Rosie. He studied his stepfather's face and noticed the new lines in it, and the dark circles beneath his blue eyes.

"What is it?" he asked, because something else was going on; something else had rattled the chief. And Parker hoped it didn't have anything to do with his mother.

"Ms. Gerber requesting the bank records of the correction officers at the jail got me thinking," Woodrow said.

"You had her request subpoenas for the bank records of all your officers?" Parker asked.

Woodrow chuckled. "It would take a long time to run all of those," he said. "And it may come down to that eventually, but for the moment I was just concerned about one."

"Spencer Dubridge?" Parker asked. The detective could be a jerk, especially to Keeli, but he was a good cop.

Woodrow shook his head. "No. The young officer who was assigned to protect Rosie."

"The one who got knocked out the night Clint saved her at her apartment?" Wasn't that what had happened?

Woodrow nodded. "Officer Maynard. I couldn't get access to his medical records to find out if he really sustained a concussion like he claimed." His blue eyes twinkled slightly. "Well, I couldn't *legally* get access even with a court order."

Parker grinned. "Nikki." There was no computer system his sister couldn't hack.

That was another reason he and Logan had kept her chained to a desk. She worked magic at a keyboard, conjuring up whatever information they had needed.

"He didn't have a concussion," the chief shared with him. "The doctor even noted that he doubted the officer had ever lost consciousness."

"So then where the hell was he when Clint and Rosie were getting shot at?" Parker asked, his temper heating up as he thought of Clint facing all those gunmen alone.

The situation had been so desperate that he'd been forced to jump out a third-story window with the witness. He was lucky that all he'd hurt was his shoulder. He could have broken his damn neck.

Woodrow shook his head. "I would have speculated that since he's a rookie, he just might have gotten scared and run off."

It happened sometimes with rookies. Despite all their training, they weren't prepared enough to deal with the real thing.

"But then you got his bank records," Parker surmised.

"He got a big influx of cash right around the time he started requesting Ms. Mendez's protection detail."

Parker cursed.

"Yeah," Woodrow said. "She's lucky to be alive given all the opportunities he had to take her out."

"But then he wouldn't have had anyone else to blame it on," Parker said. So now that the Payne Protection Agency was responsible for guarding her, he was going to no doubt try again. "Did you pick him up?"

"There's a warrant out to bring him in for questioning," Woodrow said.

Parker tilted his head.

"Nobody's picked him up yet."

Cops didn't like arresting other cops, even if they were dirty. So Officer Maynard was running around out there with his gun and his badge. If he had found Rosie before Clint had, she would have gone with him. Since he'd protected her before, she would trust him.

And it would be the last thing she ever did.

Parker couldn't help but think that Rosie's luck might have run out, and Clint's along with it.

Chapter 24

She should tell him she loved him. Rosie had been about to explain to Clint why she'd changed her mind about testifying, that she had done it for him, when the officer had told her to shut up. The barrel of his gun pinched the skin of her temple and made her head pound, he had it pressed so tightly against her.

She should tell Clint, though…because she was worried she might not have the chance if she didn't do it now. And then, before she could open her mouth, the gun blasted.

And she dropped to the ground. She felt no pain, though. She felt nothing but the weight of the officer's body on her back. Had he knocked her down?

Had he changed his mind about killing her?

From what he'd been saying, she wouldn't have thought so. She drew in a deep breath and opened her eyes. But then she wished she hadn't when she screamed at the horror she saw.

Even if she hadn't been a nurse, she would have known there was no way to treat Officer Maynard's injury.

He was dead.

What about Clint? Had the officer fired at him first?

"Clint!" she yelled for him.

Had the officer turned his weapon on her bodyguard instead of her? It would have been the smart thing to do. If he killed Clint first, he would have had a chance of getting away with murder.

Or at least his life…

But he had not managed that. She shuddered and looked away from him, trying to see around him for Clint. Had he managed to take Clint's life before losing his?

If he had…it was all her fault. She shouldn't have left the safe house. She should have never trusted Luther Mills to keep his word.

"Clint!" she called out again as she tried to wriggle from beneath the dead weight of Officer Maynard's bloodied body. But then she was free, the body rolled off her.

She hadn't done it. She hadn't had the strength. And Officer Maynard certainly hadn't moved himself.

Then strong hands reached out for her, helping her to her feet. She felt the tremor in those hands, though. And as she stared up into Clint's face, she saw that he was as shaken as she was.

"I'm sorry," she said, her voice cracking with regret. "I'm so sorry…"

Clint shook his head. "I thought he shot you." And

he pulled her against his tense body and wrapped his arms around her.

She shuddered. "I thought he had, too." And if she'd died, Clint never would have known how she felt about him. Instead he would have probably just piled more guilt on himself, assuming responsibility for her death like he had for her brother's.

She glanced down at Javier's grave. Officer Maynard's blood had spattered the small marker. But that young man's blood wasn't on Javier.

Or on Clint.

He obviously didn't feel that way, though, because he murmured, "I didn't want to have to kill him."

"I know," she said. "You tried to talk him down."

"But he was so desperate."

Luther had that effect on people, like the kid with the knife in the hospital ER. He'd been so scared.

"It's not your fault," Rosie assured him. "His blood is on Luther's hands. And so is Javier's." She stepped back and grabbed his hands, holding them in hers. "Javier's death was not your fault either."

But he just shook his head, unwilling to accept her absolution. Before she could say anything more, she heard the whine of sirens.

Someone must have reported the shots. Or maybe they'd heard the earlier arguing and had called in the disturbance. She wasn't the only one who visited her loved one's grave. Someone else was usually in the cemetery.

"We need to get out of here," Clint said, his voice gruff with urgency.

"What—why?"

"Do you think Maynard was the only cop on Luther's payroll?" he asked.

She shuddered as she considered the implications of that. They could not trust anyone.

"They could shoot us and claim it was self-defense," Clint said, spelling out one of those implications to her. "That was probably what Officer Maynard had intended to claim."

Her stomach lurched more than it had at the sight of the young officer's head wound. "What are we going to do?" she asked.

He put his arm around her waist, nearly dragging her along with him as he hurried away from Javier's grave and Officer Maynard's dead body.

"We're going to run," he told her.

Her legs were too shaky yet for running, but Clint nearly carried her along with him to the SUV he'd parked on the other side of the cemetery from the parking lot. He must have jumped the fence because there was no gate back here.

And Rosie, in her long dress, wasn't certain how she could get over the tall barrier of wrought iron. But then Clint lifted her and boosted her over it. She nearly fell onto the sidewalk on the other side. But then he was there, steadying her before she even hit the concrete.

He clicked the locks for the SUV and pulled open the passenger door. "We have to hurry," he told her, his voice full of urgency.

"But we're leaving a crime scene." Of course it wasn't the first time they'd done that. They'd left her apartment and the shoot-out at the safe house. But those times they'd been in imminent danger.

They wouldn't be able to claim that this time.

"We don't know for certain that the officers coming here work for Luther," she said. "He can't have gotten to everyone." At least she hoped he hadn't. But maybe she was being naive.

Clint must have thought so because he started the SUV and pulled away from the curb. "We can't take the chance." He glanced across the console at her. "I won't take the chance." There was such intensity in his deep green eyes, such a look of...

Her breath caught. No. It couldn't be.

She had let herself hope before that her refusing to testify would keep her and Clint safe. Now she knew it was safer to hope for nothing.

Then she wouldn't be disappointed.

Or dead.

Clint forced himself to turn away from Rosie and focus on driving. He needed to get her away from the cemetery, away from anyone else who might be on Luther Mills's payroll. And that could be anyone.

He doubted that young officer had sought out Luther on his own. Someone must have reached out to him, someone from within the department. So there had to be someone higher up working with Luther, someone high enough up that they'd found out about the Payne Protection Agency and their safe houses.

He should have tried to get more information out of Maynard. But there had been no time. He'd been too determined to carry out Luther Mills's order to kill the witness.

It didn't matter that Rosie had told him she wouldn't testify. Luther wouldn't stop trying to have her killed until she was dead.

If anything happened to Rosie, it would kill Clint, too. For those few short seconds before she'd screamed, he'd thought the officer might have shot her. And for those few seconds, it had felt as if his heart had stopped beating. As if it had just been beating for her.

He could not lose her.

So he pressed harder on the accelerator and sped off. He had no idea where he was going, just that he needed to get her as far from River City and Luther Mills's ever-expanding crew as he could.

"Won't we get in trouble for leaving the scene?" she asked. "This isn't like the other times when people were shooting at us."

"We would have gotten in more trouble if we had stayed," he pointed out. They could get dead. "People might have started shooting at us then."

"But won't they think you killed a cop?" she asked, and her brown eyes were wide with fear. "What if they don't know that he was working with Luther?"

Clint shrugged. He didn't care. All he cared about was keeping her safe.

So he could trust no one, not with Rosie's life. It—she—meant way too much to him. She meant everything to him.

"We need to go to the police department," she told him, and she reached across the console to grasp his arm. "We need to talk to the chief."

He sighed. "Usually you want me to go to hospital."

She tensed and asked, her voice cracking with alarm, "Are you hurt? Did he shoot you before he fell?"

Clint shook his head. "No, this time I'm fine." But he wasn't unscathed. He hadn't wanted to kill the young man. If only he could have talked him into putting down the gun. But Officer Maynard had been beyond reason. There was no way Clint could have reached him.

If the rest of Luther's crew were as desperate to carry out his orders, how the hell was he going to keep her safe?

Clint shuddered. "I won't be fine, though, and neither will you if we don't get the hell out of River City."

"That's what I intended to do," she told him, but she sounded regretful. "I came to Javier's grave to say goodbye. Then I realized how wrong it would be for me to run."

"Rosie..." Her instincts had been the right ones.

"We need to talk to either the chief or Jocelyn Gerber. Which one do you trust?"

"No one," he said.

"Not even me?"

"You sneaked out on me," he reminded her. And he shuddered at the thought of what could have happened to her, what nearly had happened to her. "That could have been you back there—" with that horrible head wound "—not Maynard."

"I know," she said quietly, and there was regret in her voice. "I know."

He sighed. "Damn it."

"What?" She looked behind them. "Are we being followed?"

"No..." He had cursed because he couldn't refuse her anything. He would talk to the chief, but on his terms. And only because it would be easier for them to get away—far away—from River City if they weren't wanted for the murder of a police officer.

She was right. Clint needed to explain what had happened. And then he had to make sure that it never happened again.

* * *

Woodrow was always happy to come home to his beautiful bride. No matter what was going on with the department, or with their family, she always made him feel better. Just having her at his side, a true partner and soul mate, made his life so much better than he could have ever imagined it would be.

But when he pulled into the driveway of their farmhouse in the country outside River City, there was a black SUV already parked in the drive. They had company.

It could have been any one of their children. All the Payne Protection Agencies used black SUVs. Hell, it could have even been someone from Woodrow's FBI past who was visiting. But the plate on the back bumper of the SUV wasn't a government one. It was a Michigan one.

Woodrow picked up the bouquet of flowers from the passenger seat and pushed open his door. He loved bringing his wife presents. Not that he often surprised her.

She had that innate ability of hers where she always seemed to know what he was up to. Maybe it was because they were so connected. Or maybe she was the psychic that most of their family thought she was.

When he walked inside, he found the house empty. Even though the smell of dinner wafted from the Crock-Pot on the counter, he knew she wasn't in the house because he didn't feel the vibrancy of her presence.

Then the sound of voices drew him toward the back patio. She sat at the glass-topped iron table, pouring ice tea for her guests. And his breath shuddered out in relief when he saw who they were.

"Thank God," he murmured. "You're alive."

Rosie Mendez trembled and murmured, "Barely. If Clint hadn't shown up when he did…"

Penny reached across the table and squeezed the young woman's hand. Her heart was so big; he knew she'd probably already taken Rosie and Clint into it as she had so many others over the years.

"*Your* officer would have killed her," Clint told him.

Woodrow flinched.

And Penny jumped to his defense. "Woodrow is still cleaning up the department. Our son Nicholas made a good start, but he wasn't able to get every corrupt officer off the force."

"I don't think Maynard was even on the force when Nick was chief," Clint said.

"He wasn't," Woodrow admitted. He appreciated his wife's coming to his defense. But he deserved the blame for this. "I'm the one responsible for hiring him and ultimately the one responsible for his death."

"So you know he's dead?" Clint asked, and then admitted, "I'm the one who pulled the trigger." And he sounded regretful that he'd had to.

"You had no choice," Rosie said, jumping to her bodyguard's defense just as quickly as Penny had jumped to his.

Clint Quarters was more than just a bodyguard to Ms. Mendez. And Woodrow didn't need a recording of the jailhouse visit to guess why she had gone to visit Luther Mills.

"He was going to kill me," she said, and her voice cracked with the fear she must have felt. "He would have killed us both. You had no choice, Clint. Don't you dare blame yourself." She turned toward the chief. "Please don't press charges against him. It was self-defense as well as defense of me."

Woodrow glanced over at his wife, sharing a significant look with her. Unlike the rest of the Payne family, Penny had never been involved in the bodyguard business. She was a wedding planner with a full-service venue she operated from an old chapel she'd bought years ago.

She possessed an uncanny ability to predict lasting love. Unfortunately, she had the same ability to predict danger.

"I'm not here to turn myself in to you," Clint said. "I have to be the one to protect Rosie. We can't trust anyone else."

"You can trust the Payne Protection Agency," Woodrow said, as Penny opened her mouth to probably tell him the same thing. "They're your friends."

Clint shrugged. "That's what I thought, but how the hell does Luther's crew keep finding our safe houses?"

"They've been used before," Penny said. She might not work the bodyguard business with her children, but she knew it well. Better than Woodrow did. "There have been previous incidents at them, incidents about which there would have been police reports."

She was as brilliant as she was beautiful.

"So someone could have looked up old police reports regarding the Payne Protection Agency and found out about the safe houses," Woodrow deduced.

"Someone within the department," Clint added.

He shook his head. "Not anymore. With the Freedom of Information Act, anyone can request copies of police reports. Hell, Luther Mills could have gotten the copies himself." And Woodrow wouldn't have put it past him. The drug dealer was smart, or he wouldn't have been in business as long as he had.

Rosie shuddered. And Woodrow silently berated himself. He hadn't wanted to scare her any more than she already was.

"I'm not going to arrest you," Woodrow assured Clint and Rosie. "And the district attorney's office already ruled it self-defense. We'd just discovered that Maynard was complicit in the attempt on your life at your apartment."

"Can you prove it was Luther?" Clint asked. "I can testify to what he told us."

But a good defense lawyer would tear it apart as hearsay, and Luther Mills had hired the best.

"I will testify, too," Rosie said. "About today and about my brother's murder."

"You changed your mind?" Clint asked in surprise.

And was it disappointment or fear that crossed his face? Woodrow couldn't tell, but he would ask Penny later. She would know.

"You changed my mind," Rosie told Clint. "Like you said, Javier deserves justice."

"We'll get justice for your brother," Woodrow assured her. "And we'll keep you safe."

Clint grimaced. He clearly didn't believe him.

Woodrow was just happy that the bodyguard had trusted him enough to come to him. In his shoes, he wasn't certain he would have trusted him—not if Penny's life had been the one in jeopardy.

"I have a place you two can go," he said. "A place nobody knows about."

Penny looked at him. "You do?"

"It was going to be a surprise." Along with the yellow roses, he'd intended to tell her about the cottage he'd bought for them, a place where they could go and unwind from their busy lives.

She smiled. "You spoil me."

"You deserve it," he said. She'd worked so hard for so many years to support her family after her first husband's death. Woodrow wanted to take care of her now.

"We can't use your place," Rosie said. "It's too special."

Penny squeezed the younger woman's hand. "It will be even more special to us now because it will be a place where you will be safe."

Rosie blinked furiously, as if fighting back tears. The young woman was so tough, but Penny had touched her—as she did everyone she met.

Woodrow pulled a key from his pocket and handed it over to Clint as he gave him the address and directions to the cottage. "Use it. You'll be safe there. I won't even tell anyone else where you are."

"I just went grocery shopping," Penny said as she rose from the patio table. "I filled the refrigerator and the freezer, so I can stock you up so you won't need to stop anywhere for supplies."

"I already stocked the cottage," Woodrow said, and smiled at his bride, who always thought like he did. "You two will be set until the trial."

"Thank you," Rosie said.

But Clint didn't seem as grateful. Had he had other plans about how to protect the witness?

"It's safe," Woodrow assured him again. "Nobody will find you two there."

He wasn't sure that Clint trusted him enough to believe that the cottage was safe.

And Woodrow wasn't sure that he trusted Clint now to actually take her to the cottage. From personal experience, he knew a man would do anything to protect the woman he loved. He'd taken a bullet for Penny before they'd ever gone on their first date.

Hell, he'd proposed before that first date as well. He hadn't had to date Penny to know she was an incredible woman. And maybe she'd worn off on him, because he was starting to become a hopeless romantic like her.

He hoped Rosie Mendez would someday wear Clint's ring like Penny wore his.

But first they had to survive until Luther Mills was put away for life.

Chapter 25

Rosie chuckled as she helped Clint unload the car. "Do you think she packed enough stuff for us?"

Despite the chief's saying he'd stocked the cottage already, his wife had insisted on loading them up with extra food. They'd also traded vehicles with them, so no one would spot the signature Payne Protection black SUV.

Penny Payne-Lynch had given them the keys to her station wagon and Woodrow had given them the keys to the love nest he'd bought for his new bride.

"I didn't think people like them existed," she said. "They're so generous and loving."

Especially with each other. She'd never witnessed a love like theirs before, even in the ER when people brought in their loved ones to be treated.

Clint nodded. He had been tense and quiet even after they'd left the chief's house.

"He absolved you of any blame in the shooting," she reminded Clint.

But that didn't mean that he wasn't still blaming himself—like he had over Javier's death. She closed the back door of the station wagon as he carried in the last box of food.

"What's wrong?" she asked.

The little yellow cottage was beautiful, with a wall of windows that looked out onto a nearly private lake. Only a few other houses had frontage on it, and they seemed far away and deserted on the other side of the big body of water. Nobody would find them here. She expelled a ragged breath; finally she felt safe.

From death.

But not from heartbreak.

She wasn't so certain that still would not happen. What if Clint didn't return her feelings? What if she'd only imagined that look she'd seen in his eyes back at the cemetery?

"Why?" he asked.

Apparently, he still hadn't forgiven her for changing her mind about testifying even after she'd changed it back.

Now was not the time to worry about her pride. She'd almost lost the chance to tell him how she felt about him. Even if he didn't return those feelings, she wanted him to know.

"I did it for you," she said.

His green eyes widened with shock. "How is that?"

"I went to see Luther to strike a deal with him," she explained. "I told him that I wouldn't testify if he would leave you alone. I didn't want you getting hurt anymore because of me."

"Why?" he asked again.

And here it was, the moment of truth for her. She drew in a deep breath before releasing it in a shaky sigh. "Because I love you."

He shook his head. "No, you hate me."

"I wanted to hate you," she admitted. "But then I got to know you the past few days, and I realized I didn't hate you at all. Ever…"

"But Javier—"

"What happened to Javier was not your fault," she said. "I was wrong to blame you for it. I was just so upset that he was gone. I was so full of anger, but I turned that anger on the wrong person."

He shook his head. "No, you didn't. I am to blame for his death."

"Luther Mills is to blame," she said. "And I never should have offered not to testify against him. But I was so worried. You kept getting hurt. And that last time…" She shuddered as she remembered thinking that he was gone. "You and Parker could have been killed."

Would have been—if Clint had not reacted so quickly.

Tears rushed to her eyes, blurring her vision, so that she couldn't even see his handsome face anymore. She blinked away the tears and said, "I couldn't risk losing you."

"You won't," he said. And he closed his arms around her. "You won't lose me."

Rosie reached up and looped her arms around his neck, pulling his head down to hers. Then she kissed him hungrily. They had come so close to dying only a short while ago.

So close to never being able to be together again.

She couldn't wait to be with him—in every way. Even as she moved her lips over his, she reached for his shirt, trying to pull it up.

He wasn't wearing his holster. He'd taken to tucking his gun into the back of his jeans. She remembered that moment he'd approached her and Officer Maynard with his hands empty and at his sides.

She had thought that he was unarmed. She'd thought he was going to die. Tears stung her eyes again. "I can't lose you," she murmured.

She'd already lost one man she loved. She couldn't lose another.

"Shh, don't worry about me. I'm not going anywhere." he assured her. And then he kissed her back, just as hungrily as she'd kissed him. He moved his hands from her back over the curve of her hips to the hem of her long dress. He pulled it up and over her head until she stood before him in just her underwear. These were borrowed from one of the safe houses. Just plain beige satin, but he gasped as if she were wearing fancy lingerie. "You are so beautiful," he murmured. "So damn beautiful."

She had never considered herself anything special—until now. Until the way that Clint looked at her like he had in the SUV, with such intensity in his eyes. With such emotion.

He said nothing more, just picked her up and carried her through one of the doors off the living area of the cottage. The bedroom was bright and light, too, with shimmery sheer curtains at the window and creamy yellow sheets on the bed. Then she was on the bed, too, as he lowered her to it.

But instead of joining her, he stepped back and to her

relief, finished undressing. Then he stood before her, gloriously naked but for the bandage on his shoulder.

It was still a crisp white. He had stopped bleeding. He was healing.

And finally, so had Rosie. She'd let go of the anger over Javier's death. And while she would always miss him and regret his loss, she knew she would be able to be happy again—like he'd wanted her to be…with Clint.

She reached out for him. But he stayed standing for another long moment, just staring down at her. And that look on his face…

She shivered, but it was a delicious shiver, one that had her skin tingling and her heart racing. "Clint."

He didn't join her, though. Instead he dropped to his knees next to the bed. But he leaned over and kissed her. And as he kissed her deeply, sliding his tongue between her lips, his hands moved over her body.

He traced every curve before removing her underwear. Then he traced those curves all over again.

Rosie's skin tingled everywhere he touched, and tension began to build inside her. She needed him to be closer. She needed him inside her.

She reached for him, sliding her palms over his chest to his back. Muscles rippled beneath her touch. But he stayed on his knees beside the bed. And he continued to focus on her. He replaced his hands with his mouth, kissing all the curves he'd just caressed.

He closed his lips over one nipple, tugging at it gently until she cried out at the pleasure. Then he moved his mouth lower, over her stomach to the small mound between her legs. And he made love to her with his mouth.

She arched and writhed on the bed, desperate for release—which he gave her with shattering intensity.

She cried out again, screaming his name. But it wasn't enough yet. She still ached inside—for him.

Then he was there. After rolling on a condom, he finally joined her on the bed, and he joined their bodies. She lifted her legs and arched her hips, taking him as deeply as she could. He was so big…yet he fit inside her as if they were meant for each other.

She realized now that they were. She locked her arms and legs around him, but he turned, flipping onto his back so that she straddled him. She squealed in delight as he moved even deeper inside her.

Then he locked his hands around her hips, and together they found a rhythm. She rocked back and forth, up and down, building that tension inside her again.

Sweat beaded on his lip and glistened on his muscular chest. She braced her hands against it and moved faster. His hands clenched her hips, but he didn't still her movements. He helped her, and together they found release—each tensing as the orgasms rushed through them. Spent and satiated, Rosie collapsed on his chest.

"Staying here until the trial won't be so bad," she murmured. Not if they spent all their time like this.

But Clint, still clutching her hips, lifted her away from him. And as he got out of bed, he said, "We're not staying here."

"But the chief assured us it's safe."

"We're leaving," Clint said. "And we're not coming back for the trial."

He walked away, leaving her in shock as he stepped into the bathroom. What the hell was going on?

He'd wanted her to testify. He'd been angry when she'd told the assistant district attorney that she wasn't going to. Why had he changed his mind?

* * *

When Clint stepped out of the bathroom, he found Rosie exactly how he'd left her, sitting up in bed with a stunned expression on her beautiful face. He wanted to crawl back in that bed with her, wanted to pull her naked body into his arms and hold her all night.

But instead he picked up his clothes from the floor. "We need to get out of here, as far away from River City as we can get."

They could leave the country. That would be the smart thing to do. That would get them outside of Luther Mills's reach. It would have to.

"I don't understand," she said. "You were mad when I changed my mind."

Clint still couldn't believe she'd done that for him—because she loved him. How was that possible? No matter what she said, he was responsible for her brother's death. He'd thought she would never forgive him, let alone fall in love with him.

"I didn't know why you were doing it," he said. "And I didn't realize—until Officer Maynard said it—how stupid it was to expect you to testify."

She shook her head. "It's not stupid. It's the right thing to do—for Javier."

He hated that she'd thrown his words back at him. "Javier made me promise to keep you safe," he said. "This is the only way I can do that, by not letting you testify."

"Is that the only reason you want to keep me safe?" she asked. "Because of your promise to my brother?"

He shook his head. "No. It's because I love you, and I don't want to lose you."

Her brown eyes widened. "You love me?"

He snorted at her surprise. "I loved you from the

first moment Javier introduced us. You are so beautiful, but more than that you're smart and strong and loyal and fierce—"

She jumped up from the bed and threw her arms around his neck, pulling his head down for her kiss. She kissed him passionately before breaking away to murmur, "You love me..."

"Yes," he said. "That's why I can't risk you testifying." He shuddered as he remembered everything Officer Maynard had said. "It's too risky."

"Not with you by my side," she said. "You've saved me over and over again. You will keep me safe during the trial. And until the trial, we will be safe here together."

"But if something happened to you..." He would never forgive himself.

"It wouldn't be your fault," she said. "Just like Javier's death wasn't your fault. It was Luther's. And he needs to pay for that. He needs to be put away in such a high-security prison that he will never be able to hurt anyone else."

She was right.

"Damn you," he murmured.

And she laughed. "You know it's the right thing to do. For Javier, for your cousin..."

He nodded.

"But it means so much to know that you would put me before them," she said. "Before justice." She blinked back the tears brimming in her beautiful eyes. "I have never been loved like you love me."

He shook his head. "Your brother loved you. He wanted to make you proud."

The tears spilled over. "He did. He did make me

proud." Her breath hitched, and Clint pulled her close again, holding her as she cried for Javier.

But she didn't cry long before she pulled back. And she was smiling again. "You're not the only one he got a promise out of before he died."

Clint furrowed his brow as he stared down at her. What could Javier had wanted from her? He'd said she'd already given him everything. "What?" he asked.

"He used his last breath to tell me that you and I belong together," she said, her voice cracking with emotion. "He made me promise to give you a chance."

"Instead you told me to go to hell," he reminded her.

"I'm stubborn."

"Don't I know it," he murmured. But it was that obstinacy that had kept her in school and then college. She'd worked hard, but it was her perseverance that had ensured her success.

"Will you honor his promise now?" Clint asked. "Will you give me a chance?"

"Yes," she said. "I think Javier was right. I think we do belong together."

Javier was right. But Clint had always known it, too. And he would do his best to honor his promise to her brother. He would keep her safe...for the rest of their lives.

"What the hell do you mean?" Luther shouted into the cell phone. He didn't care who overheard him talking. Sure, the guards were getting nervous. They knew they were being investigated. But if they didn't do what he wanted, he'd threatened that he would help the assistant DA with her little investigation.

"We can't find the witness or Clint Quarters anywhere," the man replied.

This was the man—the one high enough up to give Luther the information he needed. Until now.

"You have to know," Luther insisted.

Was this man getting nervous, too—like the correction officers were?

Did he think their alliance was about to be discovered? Luther had other sources, but this was the guy who'd found the Payne Protection Agency safe houses. This was the one he needed the most.

"I don't think anybody knows where he took her," the guy insisted.

Luther snorted. "They couldn't have just disappeared."

"Looks like that's exactly what happened."

"Clint Quarters is just a bodyguard now. Rosie just a nurse. They would need to use credit cards or at least make withdrawals from their savings." They couldn't live off love. The thought sickened Luther. "You must be able to track down where they are."

"I tried. There's been no activity on any of their accounts. Are you sure they're not dead?"

"Yes." If someone had offed them, that person would have been bragging to Luther for respect and begging for the big reward he'd offered. "You need to keep looking."

"I will."

But it was clear he wasn't hopeful that he'd find them. Maybe that was good, though. Maybe they'd run away and Rosie really had no intention of testifying against him.

Of course Luther still wanted her dead and Clint

Quarters deader than dead. But he would worry about that later. Right now he had to shift his focus.

"That crime scene tech has to go next," Luther said. "She's not been as easily intimidated as I'd thought she would be."

None of them had been, though.

Did they not realize who they were dealing with? Luther Mills never lost.

"Wendy Thompson has a Payne Protection bodyguard, too," he was warned.

"Who?"

"Hart Fisher."

Luther laughed. Another former vice cop. Another officer who had quit because he hadn't been able to get him.

This was going to be fun...

* * * * *

Don't miss out on any of the
Bachelor Bodyguards in Lisa Childs's
heart racing miniseries:

Soldier Bodyguard
In the Bodyguard's Arms
Single Mom's Bodyguard
Nanny Bodyguard

Available now from
Harlequin Romantic Suspense!

COMING NEXT MONTH FROM

◆ HARLEQUIN®

ROMANTIC suspense

Available March 5, 2019

#2031 COLTON'S CONVENIENT BRIDE
The Coltons of Roaring Springs
by Jennifer Morey
Decker Colton agreed to an arranged marriage but when his new bride, Kendall Hadley, is nearly kidnapped, they'll have to dodge danger and navigate a relationship that's gone from business deal...to pure pleasure!

#2032 COWBOY DEFENDER
Cowboys of Holiday Ranch • by Carla Cassidy
Clay Madison has set his eyes on single mom Miranda Silver, but when she's kidnapped, it becomes a race against time to save her.

#2033 SPECIAL OPS COWBOY
Midnight Pass, Texas • by Addison Fox
After a one-night stand leads to a pregnancy and with the threats against her escalating, Reese Grantham turns to Hoyt Reynolds for protection. Can he stay committed to his plan to remain unattached while keeping Reese and their baby out of the crosshairs?

#2034 TEMPTED BY THE BADGE
To Serve and Seduce • by Deborah Fletcher Mello
History teacher Joanna Barnes has been charged with a crime she didn't commit. Private investigator Mingus Black has no qualms about getting his hands dirty to prove her innocence— but more than his career is at risk now...

YOU CAN FIND MORE INFORMATION ON UPCOMING HARLEQUIN® TITLES, FREE EXCERPTS AND MORE AT WWW.HARLEQUIN.COM.

Get 4 FREE REWARDS!

We'll send you 2 FREE Books <u>plus</u> 2 FREE Mystery Gifts.

Harlequin® Romantic Suspense books feature heart-racing sensuality and the promise of a sweeping romance set against the backdrop of suspense.

FREE Value Over **$20**

YES! Please send me 2 FREE Harlequin® Romantic Suspense novels and my 2 FREE gifts (gifts are worth about $10 retail). After receiving them, if I don't wish to receive any more books, I can return the shipping statement marked "cancel." If I don't cancel, I will receive 4 brand-new novels every month and be billed just $4.99 per book in the U.S. or $5.74 per book in Canada. That's a savings of at least 12% off the cover price! It's quite a bargain! Shipping and handling is just 50¢ per book in the U.S. and 75¢ per book in Canada.* I understand that accepting the 2 free books and gifts places me under no obligation to buy anything. I can always return a shipment and cancel at any time. The free books and gifts are mine to keep no matter what I decide.

240/340 HDN GMYZ

Name (please print)

Address   Apt. #

City   State/Province   Zip/Postal Code

Mail to the **Reader Service:**
IN U.S.A.: P.O. Box 1341, Buffalo, NY 14240-8531
IN CANADA: P.O. Box 603, Fort Erie, Ontario L2A 5X3

Want to try 2 free books from another series! Call 1-800-873-8635 or visit www.ReaderService.com.

The silence on the car ride to the public hearing at the Chicago
Board of Education building on Madison Street was jaw-dropping.
Mingus maneuvered his car through traffic, his expression smug
as he stole occasional glances in her direction. Joanna stared out
the passenger-side window, still lost in the heat of Mingus's touch.
That kiss had left her shaking, her knees quivering and her heart
racing. She couldn't not think about it if she wanted to.

His kiss had been everything she'd imagined and more. It
was summer rain in a blue sky, fudge cake with scoops of praline
ice cream, balloons floating against a backdrop of clouds, small
puppies, bubbles in a spa bath and fireworks over Lake Michigan.
It had left her completely satiated and famished for more. Closing
her eyes and kissing him back had been as natural as breathing.
And there was no denying that she had kissed him back. She hadn't
been able to speak since, no words coming that would explain the
wealth of emotion flowing like a tidal wave through her spirit.

They paused at a red light. Mingus checked his mirrors and
the flow of traffic as he waited for his turn to proceed through

the intersection. Joanna suddenly reached out her hand for his, entwining his fingers between her own.

"I'm still mad at you," Joanna said.

"I know. I'm still mad at myself. I just felt like I was failing you. You need results and I'm not coming up with anything concrete. I want to fix this and suddenly I didn't know if I could. I felt like I was being outwitted. Like someone's playing this game better than I am, but it's not a game. They're playing with your life, and I don't plan to let them beat either one of us."

"From day one you believed me. Most didn't and, to be honest, I don't know that anyone else does. But not once have you looked at me like I'm lying or I'm crazy. This afternoon, you yelling at me felt like doubt, and I couldn't handle you doubting me. It broke my heart."

Mingus squeezed her fingers, still stalled at the light, a line of cars beginning to pull in behind him. "I don't doubt you, baby. But we need to figure this out and, frankly, we're running out of time."

The honking of a car horn yanked his attention back to the road. He pulled into the intersection and turned left. Minutes later he slid into a parking spot and shut down the car engine. Joanna was still staring out the window.

"Are you okay?" he asked.

Joanna nodded and gave him her sweetest smile. "Yeah. I was just thinking that I really like it when you call me 'baby.'"

Don't miss
Tempted by the Badge *by Deborah Fletcher Mello,*
available March 2019 wherever
Harlequin® Romantic Suspense books
and ebooks are sold.

www.Harlequin.com

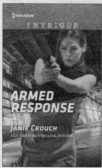

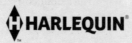

Love Harlequin romance?

DISCOVER.

Be the first to find out about promotions, news and exclusive content!

Facebook.com/HarlequinBooks

Twitter.com/HarlequinBooks

Instagram.com/HarlequinBooks

Pinterest.com/HarlequinBooks

ReaderService.com

EXPLORE.

Sign up for the Harlequin e-newsletter and download a free book from any series at **TryHarlequin.com.**

CONNECT.

Join our Harlequin community to share your thoughts and connect with other romance readers!
Facebook.com/groups/HarlequinConnection

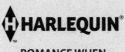

HARLEQUIN®

ROMANCE WHEN YOU NEED IT